Braving the North Atlantic

The Vikings, the Cabots, and Jacques Cartier Voyage to America

BY DELNO C. WEST
AND JEAN M. WEST

ILLUSTRATED WITH PRINTS, MAPS, AND PHOTOGRAPHS

ATHENEUM BOOKS FOR YOUNG READERS

THIS BOOK IS DEDICATED TO OUR CHILDREN

Douglas J. West

Scott and Delisa Stroming

Dawn West Corbally

John and Rose Hawke

Atheneum Books for Young Readers

An imprint of Simon & Schuster Children's Publishing Division

1230 Avenue of the Americas

New York, New York 10020

Book design by Edward Miller

The text of this book is set in New Caledonia

First Edition

Printed in the United States of America

10 9 8 7 6 5 4 3 2 1

Library of Congress Cataloging-in-Publication Data

West, Delno C., 1936—

Braving the North Atlantic : the Vikings, the Cabots, and Jacques Cartier

voyage to America / by Delno C. West and Jean M. West.—1st. ed.

p.   cm.

Includes index.

Summary: Covers the discovery and exploration of North America by a variety of
European explorers.

ISBN 0-689-31822-7

1. America—Discovery and exploration—Juvenile literature. [1. America—Discovery and
exploration.] I. West, Jean M. II. Title.

E101.W47   1996   970.01—dc20   95-43140   CIP   AC

TABLE OF CONTENTS

CHRONOLOGY

12,000 B.C.	Asian peoples first arrive on North American continent, coming across the Bering land bridge from Siberia. Date is approximate and according to general consensus of modern archaeologists.
A.D. 550	Voyages from Ireland by St. Brendan. Date approximate.
A.D. 795	Irish monks settle in Iceland. Date approximate.
A.D. 870	Norse begin to colonize Iceland. Date approximate.
A.D. 982	Erik the Red exiled to Greenland.
A.D. 985	Bjarni Herjolfsson sights North American coast.
A.D. 1001	Leif Eriksson builds Leifsbudir in Vinland.
A.D. 1004	Thorvald Eriksson and Thorfinn Karlsefni each attempt to build a permanent settlement in Vinland.
A.D. 1492	Christopher Columbus sails across the Ocean Sea and discovers the New World in the Caribbean islands.
A.D. 1496	John Cabot's first voyage. Bad weather forces him to turn back.
A.D. 1497	John Cabot sails across the Ocean Sea to Newfoundland, thus rediscovering North America.
A.D. 1498	John Cabot's third voyage across the Ocean Sea. He, his ships, and their crews disappear.
A.D. 1500	João Fernandes attempts to sail to Newfoundland.
A.D. 1501	Gaspar Côrte Real crosses the Ocean Sea to Newfoundland. Finds natives with European artifacts.
A.D. 1501	João Fernandes crosses the Ocean Sea.
A.D. 1502	Miguel Côrte Real sails across the Ocean Sea to find his brother Gaspar, who has disappeared. Miguel also disappears.
A.D. 1502	João Fernandes makes his second voyage across the Ocean Sea to Newfoundland.

A.D. 1508	Sebastian Cabot sails across the Ocean Sea and to the north, where he probably finds Hudson Bay.
A.D. 1524	Giovanni Verrazano, in the service of France, sails across the Ocean Sea to the Outer Banks off the Carolinas. He coasts north and into New York Bay.
A.D. 1526	Sebastian Cabot sails to South America and up the Rio de la Plata.
A.D. 1534	Jacques Cartier, in the service of France, sails across the Ocean Sea to St. Lawrence Strait and on up the strait as far as Gaspé Bay.
A.D. 1535	Cartier's second voyage penetrates North America up the St. Lawrence River as far as modern-day Montreal.
A.D. 1541	Cartier's third and final voyage to North America, again sailing up the St. Lawrence River to slightly beyond modern-day Montreal.
A.D. 1576	Martin Frobisher's first voyage to the New World.
A.D. 1577	Martin Frobisher's second voyage to the New World.
A.D. 1578	Martin Frobisher's third voyage to the New World.
A.D. 1607	Henry Hudson's first voyage.
A.D. 1609	Henry Hudson's second voyage.
A.D. 1610-11	Henry Hudson's third voyage.

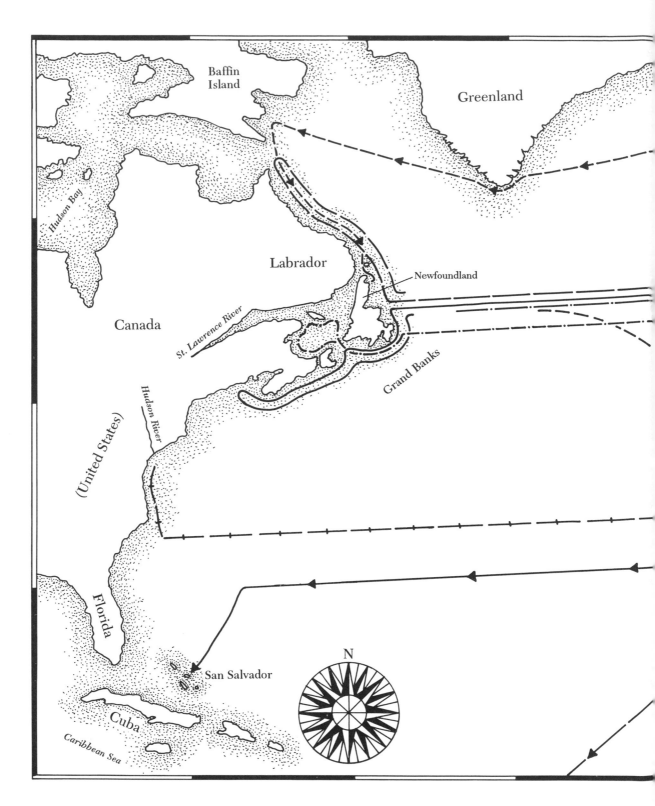

Baffin
Island

Greenland

Hudson Bay

Labrador

Newfoundland

Canada

St. Lawrence River

(United States)

Hudson River

Grand Banks

Florida

San Salvador

N

Cuba

Caribbean Sea

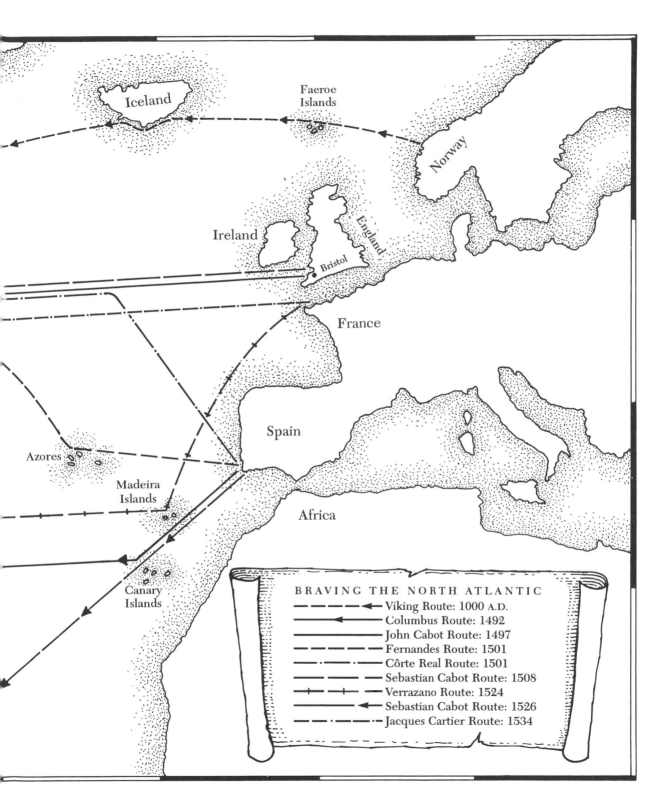

Iceland

Faeroe
Islands

Norway

Ireland

England

Bristol

France

Spain

Azores

Madeira
Islands

Africa

Canary
Islands

BRAVING THE NORTH ATLANTIC
Viking Route: 1000 A.D.
Columbus Route: 1492
John Cabot Route: 1497
Fernandes Route: 1501
Côrte Real Route: 1501
Sebastian Cabot Route: 1508
Verrazano Route: 1524
Sebastian Cabot Route: 1526
Jacques Cartier Route: 1534

I.

THE EARLIEST EXPLORATION
OF THE NORTH ATLANTIC

The first recorded European discovery of North America was by a Viking man named Bjarni Herjolfsson who was looking for his father. This strange tale is recorded for us in Viking sagas.

Iceland had been settled by hardy Scandinavians for about two hundred years when the famous Viking Erik the Red was expelled from the island around the year A.D. 982. Because he was a brawler who had killed several men, the punishment for Erik the Red was banishment from Iceland for three years. He had heard of islands to the west of Iceland reported by a Viking named Gunnbjorn, who had spotted land after being lost in a storm. Erik decided to sail into the unknown western ocean to find them, spend his exile time there, and then return to Iceland. After several days of sailing, Erik the Red came to an ice-packed, glacial coast on which it was impossible to land. A strong ocean current off that coast carried him south, along with many icebergs, until he rounded the tip of the great land and was pushed up on the western side. Finally, on the western side of the land, he ventured into several fjords, looking for grasslands where he might settle a farmstead. He found an area he liked on the southwest coast and spent his three years of exile there laying out farm sites. The area was rich in wild game and birds and the nearby sea was full of fish and edible sea mammals. The fjord he named "Eriksfjord," his homesite he called "Battahlid." Archaeological excavations of Battahlid reveal that Erik built a large and comfortable home with thick stone-and-sod walls to insulate it from the harsh winter weather.

At the end of his banishment in A.D. 985, Erik the Red returned to Iceland in order to entice more people to settle near his farmstead. The land he had settled was barren for the most part, and about seven hundred thousand square miles of it was covered by a great ice cap. Such a place would not attract many settlers, but like land promoters today, he named the new region "Greenland," which it was not, but which he was sure would appeal to prospective colonists. He was successful in luring new people to his farmstead and, according to the sagas, between twenty-five and thirty-five ships followed him back to Greenland, each crowded with men, women, children, domestic animals, and supplies.

The next summer, a viking named Bjarni Herjolfsson left Norway in his trading ship loaded with cargo for the colonies in Iceland. It was his habit to sail from Norway to Iceland every other summer with supplies, spend the winter with his father, Herjolf, who lived in Iceland, and return to Norway the next summer. But when Bjarni arrived in Iceland in the summer of 986, he found that his father had left there bound for the new colony of Greenland.

Bjarni was an experienced seaman who was successful enough to own his own ship. Still wishing to spend the winter with his father, he decided to sail on to Greenland. He had never gone there before, and he had no chart of the area, but that did not deter the young sailor. Leaving Iceland, however, he and his men became locked into heavy fog and lost their bearings. Now they were in real trouble, sailing in an unknown sea with no way to find directions. When the fog lifted days later, they found themselves in sight of land that was flat and covered with forest. Bjarni knew that this could not be Greenland, as he had been told that its coastline would rise sharply from the sea with deep fjords.

Sagas

Norse sagas (*sagas* means "tellings") were poems about the glories of the past which reached their height of popularity in the thirteenth century. Most of the stories are about individuals or families during the tenth and early eleventh centuries. They are best described as fictional "history." They do rest on a foundation of historical events, but they have been embroidered upon by the creative imaginations of storytellers, authors, transcribers, and others who interpreted the facts. Sagas also retell Old Testament stories, Christian and pagan superstitions, Norse folktales, and fables, and often contain medieval pseudoscience. Their purpose was to show the human destiny of the men and women the writer was telling about. Sagas could be shortened or lengthened; new material was added without foundation in fact; and sometimes, the point of the original story was misunderstood by a new teller or transcriber. The student of history has to be very careful using this kind of primary source. On the one hand, it is frequently the only document available, and on the other hand, it can be confusing and misleading. For example, the two sagas that tell about the voyages to Vinland contradict each other repeatedly.

Bjarni and his crew sailed along the coast until the land changed into glacier-covered mountains. His sense of the sea told him that he had sailed too far west, and the stars indicated that he was too far south. He refused to let his men go ashore anywhere along the coast he had found, and instead continued north up the coast of what we now call Labrador and eventually east into the open ocean. After four days on the open sea sailing east, he found Greenland and the place where his father lived. Thus, by accident, Bjarni was the first European of record to see the shores of North America.

Bjarni's Discovery as Told in the *Greenland Saga*

They put out the moment they were ready, and sailed for three days before losing sight of land [Iceland]. Then their following wind died down, and north winds and fogs overtook them, so that they had no idea which way they were going. This continued over many days, but eventually they saw the sun and could then get their bearings. They now hoisted sail, and sailed that day before sighting land, and debated among themselves what land this could be. To his way of thinking, said Bjarni, it could not be Greenland . . . [as it] was not mountainous and was covered with forest. . . . After this they sailed for two days before sighting another land. [In Bjarni's] opinion this was no more Greenland than the first place. . . . [It] was flat country covered with woods. . . . He gave orders to hoist sail, which was done; they turned their prow from the land and sailed out to sea three days with a southwest wind, and then they saw the third land, and this land was high, mountainous, and glaciered. . . . It was an island.

Once more they turned their prow from the land and held out to sea with the same following wind. . . . This time they sailed for four days and then saw the fourth land. . . . [They came] to land under a certain cape in the evening of the day. There was a boat on the cape, and there too on the cape lived Herjolf, Bjarni's father.[1]

1. Gwyn Jones, ed. and trans., the *Greenland Saga*. In *The Norse Atlantic Sagas* (London: Oxford University Press, 1964), 156.

In reality, the very earliest discovery of the Western Hemisphere occurred thousands of years before Bjarni's trip, when peoples from Eurasia (i.e., the land-mass of Europe and Asia combined) migrated from west to east across the Bering

Strait from what is today Siberia in Russia to Alaska. Since this happened centuries before historical records, we can only speculate from archaeological remains about who these people were and why they chose to cross the Bering Strait into the northwest corner of the Western Hemisphere. As the centuries passed, these forebears of today's Native American peoples spread out over the entire North and South American continents settling the new land. In time, their migration was forgotten on the Eurasian continent.

Although it would not be until the fifteenth century A.D. that permanent communication with these people was established by Renaissance European sailors and adventurers, brief contact may have occurred from time to time in the European Middle Ages. Unsubstantiated myth and legend tells of Irish and Welsh adventurers sailing to unknown western regions across the Ocean Sea (in the Middle Ages the Atlantic Ocean was called the Ocean Sea or the Sea of Darkness), and even more obscure myths tell of ancient Phoenician, Egyptian, Greek, and Chinese adventurers who might have landed in what today we call the Americas. Unfortunately, none of these early explorers left a record of their adventures, if indeed they ever did make the journey across the Ocean Sea.

There is some evidence that Africans may have crossed the short length of ocean between Cape Verde and the Americas using the strong north equatorial ocean current. The only testimony to this is an Arab account by Ibn Fadl Allah al-Omari, who wrote in the fourteenth century that a predecessor of the famous Emperor Kanka Musa of Mali sent two hundred ships out to cross the great ocean. None of this armada returned. These ships were probably large canoes tied together, a common form of ocean transportation in medieval Africa. Further data has been accumulated by scholars who are trying to establish early voyages by Africans to the Americas. They point out cultural parallels between African, Aztec, and Inca peoples, and numerous linguistic similarities between the Mandingoes of Africa and the Aztecs and Carib peoples.

Irish monks sailed in hide-covered rowboats to the Faeroe Islands, some two hundred miles short of Iceland, in the early Middle Ages even before the Vikings. Irish storytellers wove travel tales from such adventures to create legends about seafaring monks. The most famous is the legend of St. Brendan of Ardfert, who lived in the late fifth and early sixth centuries. The stories about St. Brendan were first told and retold. They were finally written down some three hundred years after his death, in the ninth century. Over a seven-year period, St. Brendan may have made two voyages into the North Atlantic looking for what he called the "Land of Promise," or paradise. The legend tells many details that enable us to recognize the Faeroe Islands, maybe the Azores, and Iceland. St. Brendan supposedly sailed west beyond Iceland for forty days, during which he encountered

The story of St. Brendan tells of many encounters with strange creatures in the Ocean Sea. Here the monk and his companions meet a mermaid. (British Library)

whales, icebergs, dark-skinned people, and a creature he called a "sea cat" (a walrus?). When he reached the Land of Promise, he described it as a mainland, not an island, where he spent forty days exploring. Whether the Land of Promise was what we now know as Greenland or the shores of North America continues to be a topic of debate among scholars.

Knowledge about early Irish seafaring into the North Atlantic relies on highly controversial sources. The Vikings, on the other hand, left their sagas. Although sagas cannot be considered as literal fact, they do contain grains of truth about seafaring activities some five hundred years before Columbus sailed. But besides the information contained in the Greenland sagas, there is also archaeological evidence that supports the idea of early Viking settlements in what today is Newfoundland, Canada.

The Viking voyages to North America in the tenth century would have been impossible if it were not for their ship technology. No other people in Europe had ships constructed so that they could continuously cross the ocean. Viking ships were built in different sizes and shapes for various purposes. There were ships used for coastal trade, warships, and an assortment of merchant ships. We learn something about them from three sources: underwater archaeology, the sagas, and burial mounds where famous people were entombed in ceremonial ships. Viking ships have been found as large as eighty-eight feet long and as small as rowboats. Generally speaking, Viking ships were "clinker" built, that is, with each plank on the sides overlapping the other and riveted to it. These planks were made of sturdy wood. They were fairly narrow and about one inch thick. Internally, the ship construction was formed of ribs that rested on crossbeams and was built on a foundation of a single, lengthwise beam called the keel, cut from a giant tree. The internal structure was lashed together with spruce roots or animal sinews. This was one of the major reasons why Viking ships could make long trips at sea. The lashings gave the ship flexibility and allowed its timbers to move with the huge ocean

Viking Ships

The most powerful Viking men owned ships that were built in Norway and sailed in the North Atlantic. Three huge burial mounds built by the Vikings on the coast of Oslo Fjord in Norway were each found to contain a ship. These have been excavated and can be seen at the Ship Museum on the island of Bygdoy in the Oslo Harbor. The most famous of these is the Gokstad ship unearthed in 1800 and pictured below. In a wooden chamber at the stern of the ship was buried a Viking chieftain in full dress and heavily armed. The burial dates from about A.D. 900. The Gokstad ship is 76 feet, 6 inches long and 17 feet, 6 inches wide at its greatest width. The ship is very shallow (only 6.4 feet from keel to gunwale). It had been rigged with a square sail and side rudder. Scholars believe that the Gokstad ship is similar to oceangoing vessels of the Viking era. In 1893 a replica of the Gokstad ship crossed the Atlantic to be displayed at the Chicago World Fair. The ship performed so well that it outran modern steamships of that era. These Viking ships were not only fast, they were flexible. But, since these were shallow-draft ships, the sailors preferred to stay out of storms. When a storm hit, they would sail out of its path, frequently going so far as to get lost. This is probably what happened to Bjarni when he drifted into sight of the North American coast.

(Oslo, Universitetets Oldsaksamling)

swells and not break apart under the stress. Viking ships were built for both rowing and sailing. Most would have a square sail and oars for sixteen or more men to row the boat when necessary. The shallow ship rode low in the water, so it could not only sail on the open ocean but also be beached and go up rivers. Decking varied and seemed to be highly portable. Deck planks could be removed or added as needed to store cargo or to bail out bilge water.

Once Bjarni Herjolfsson found his father, Herjolf, he had a great tale to tell about his adventure (and the tale became incorporated into the *Greenland Saga*). He told the colonists led by Erik the Red of his discovery of land to the west of Greenland. They found the story fascinating, but no one was interested in returning immediately to where Bjarni had been.

One of Erik the Red's sons, Leif Eriksson, however, heard the saga of Bjarni many times, and in A.D. 1001 he purchased Bjarni's ship. Leif Eriksson is described in the saga as a large, imposing man who was noted for dealing fairly with everyone. He gathered a crew of thirty-five sailors and set out for the lands Bjarni had encountered. Sailing due west, he and his crew made landfall where the coast was mountainous and covered with glaciers. This was probably modern-day Baffin Island, which Leif named "Helluland" (Flat-stone land). Leif and his crew realized that this territory was barren and useless, so they turned their tiny ship south, coming to a level region covered with forests. This area, which Leif named "Markland" (Woodland), is modern-day Labrador. Still not satisfied with what they had found, Leif and his party sailed even farther south, coming to a place which he named "Vinland." The exact location of Vinland has been a mystery to modern scholars. If the word means "vineland" or "wineland," then its location has to be farther south than Newfoundland, as grapes do not grow that far north. On the other hand, if Vinland means "grassland," which is another translation of the word, then the coast of Newfoundland is the probable location. Wherever it was, it was there that they built their winter campsite, which Leif named "Leifsbudir." Many

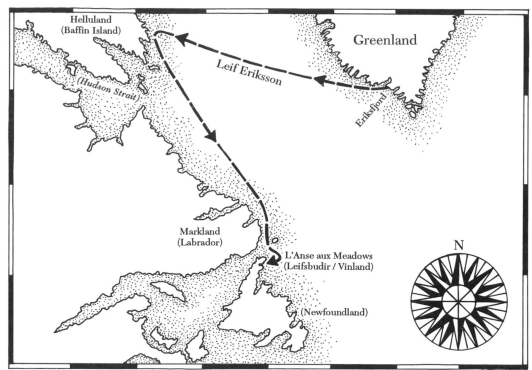

The estimated route of Leif Eriksson from Greenland to Vinland

modern scholars believe this may have been the foundation for the famous Viking archaeological site at L'Anse aux Meadows on the northeastern tip of Newfoundland.

In comparison to Greenland, from where they had come, the area called Vinland was lush. The *Greenland Saga* describes it as plentiful in fish and grass, and in *Erik the Red's Saga* wild wheat, maple trees, and grapevines are abundant. When the small party left to return to Greenland, they filled their craft with timber and filled a tow boat with grapes or berries. This last tidbit of information further confuses the location of Vinland. Could Leif Eriksson and his men have sailed farther south and gathered some sort of berry or wild grape, or could they have traded for them? Or, could the grapes or berries simply have been partridgeberries, which grow in Newfoundland? Partridgeberries have long been used to make a wine in Norway, Sweden, and Russia, where they are called lingenberries.

Leif Eriksson had every intention of returning to his encampment, but his father, Erik the Red, died, leaving Leif with family responsibilities. Leif's brother, whose name was Thorvald, wanted to see that Vinland that Leif had spoken of with such great enthusiasm. Borrowing Leif's ship, Thorvald sailed and found theencampment of Leifsbudir in Vinland. Thorvald and his men spent the summer exploring westward, and returned to winter at Leifsbudir. In the spring they sailed to explore the coast north of Vinland. Then the small ship hit stormy seas and ran aground, which ripped out its keel. This caused a delay of several weeks.

Thorvald's trip is also the first recorded incident of contact between North American native peoples and the Norsemen. Sailing on after fixing their keel, the Norsemen entered a fjord, where they found skin boats and nine native men. The

The site of the Viking settlement at L'Anse aux Meadows in Newfoundland (Canadian Park Service)

How Did Vikings
Guide Their Ships?

Vikings, people from the fjords and inlets (*viks*) of Scandinavian countries, did not have any sophisticated instruments to guide their ships. They sailed from island to island across the North Atlantic, where the islands are about 250 miles apart. Iceland to Greenland is the longest stretch, about 600 miles. Navigation depended on knowledge of the ocean and a kind of latitude sailing. Vikings could calculate their latitude by knowing the relationship between the sun or North Star and their own location. The ship's captain would put himself on a course from a site in Norway and stay on that route without changing. He stayed on track by the primitive method of observing his angle to the North Star, the sun, and the moon. This could be done by extending the arm with the thumb up toward the star or moon or by the use of a "bearing dial," pictured below. Many times ships would carry land-sighting birds, a technique as old as Noah in the Old Testament. Land-sighting birds, such as ravens, would be released when the captain became confused, and their flight toward the nearest land could reorient him. Captains also were familiar with the currents of the northern latitudes, the fish, the birds, the plants in the sea, the clouds, and the wind. It was a very crude system, but it got them to the general location of the place they were heading. When storms or fog rolled in, navigation was nearly impossible: then a sailor could only rely on a feeling for the sea and his own sense of direction. In the Icelandic *Landnamabok* (Book of Land-taking) sailors give directions on how to sail directly from Norway to Greenland, a distance of approximately 1,500 miles. The path is practical, but imprecise: "From Hernar in Norway one is to keep sailing west for Huarf in Greenland and then you will sail north of Shetland so far that you can just sight it in very clear weather; but steer south of the Faroes so that the sea appears halfway up the mountain slopes; farther on, pass south of Iceland so that you may have birds and whales from it."[2]

The bearing dial and the "sun stone" were instruments used by later Vikings, but no one knows for sure when they were first adopted. The bearing dial was a notched wooden object with a shaft through the center. The person holding it could sight it at the sun and the notches would point the pilot toward the right direction on the horizon. In a sense, it worked like a compass, as one could find north, east, south, and west from the reading. The sun stone was calcite, or Iceland spar. This is a crystal rock that changes color when held up to the sun. The tint of the crystal is different at each angle, so that the user could approximate his angle to the sun by the color of the stone and thus figure his latitude. Both of these instruments were in use among Viking sailors by the later Middle Ages, but there is no proof of their use as early as the tenth century.

2. E. G. R. Taylor, *The Heaven-Finding Art* (London: Hollis and Carter, 1956), 103.

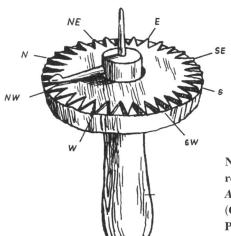

Norse bearing dial as reconstructed by Gwyn Jones, *A History of the Vikings* (Oxford: Oxford University Press, 1968, 193.)

encounter ended in a pitched battle in which eight natives were killed and one escaped. The escapee soon returned with many other natives, and even though the Norsemen were able to defend themselves and get away, Thorvald was fatally wounded by an arrow. The remaining members of the expedition returned to Greenland.

Leif Eriksson's encampment, Leifsbudir, was to see more occupation. The sagas differ in detail about the next trip to Vinland, but we will use the information recorded in the *Greenland Saga*. According to this account, a wealthy Norseman by the name of Thorfinn Karlsefni came to Greenland with a trading cargo shortly after Thorvald's men returned. Thorvald's widow, Gudrid, convinced Karlsefni to try to colonize Vinland. According to the saga, Thorfinn organized three ships to carry 250 men and women along with their equipment and

Ruins of L'Anse aux Meadows showing foundations of Viking buildings. Was this Leifsbudir? (Canadian Park Service)

L'Anse aux Meadows

The Viking presence in North America has long been a favorite theme of Scandinavian Americans, who continuously promote the idea that they were the first European immigrants to the Western Hemisphere. Some well-known archaeological sites, inscriptions, and artifacts, including the Newport, Rhode Island, Round Tower; the Kensington Stone; mooring holes; and runic inscriptions found from New England to Minnesota are based on dubious evidence, and historians are suspicious of their authenticity. The so-called Vinland Map (Historic Map 1) caused much stir in 1965, but its authenticity is at question.

There are two rather definite scraps of evidence which are accepted by scholars. One is a reference by Adam of Bremen, an eleventh-century chronicler, who tells of a discovery to the west called Wineland. The other is the archaeological site at L'Anse aux Meadows. Discovered in 1960 by Helge Ingstad and excavated under the leadership of his wife, Anne, L'Anse aux Meadows is the only identified Viking habitation found on North American soil. Helge Ingstad undertook systematic searches along the Canadian coast in 1960 by both boat and airplane. He found a group of densely overgrown houses on the northern point of Newfoundland at Epaves Bay at the small fishing village of L'Anse aux Meadows. Excavations have uncovered nine houses with hearths, cooking pits, a smithy, boathouses, bog iron (clumps of high-grade iron ore that are found in bogs), a bronze pin, and a soapstone spindle whorl (a tool used in spinning wool into thread). No one has questioned that L'Anse aux Meadows is a Viking site. The architecture is definitely Scandinavian, and carbon dating and other techniques place the buildings and artifacts during the right time period. Was this the farm settlement of Leif Eriksson? This cannot be determined for certain.

Reconstruction of Viking dwelling at L'Anse aux Meadows. Such houses were made from sod with poles for support. The sod was a good insulation, making the houses snug and warm in the winter. (Canadian Park Service)

livestock. The colonizing party reached Vinland in late summer and inhabited an area just a short distance from Leif's old camp. The first winter was mild, allowing them to settle in and build homes. Another stroke of good fortune was that they found a beached whale which they cut up for food.

Thorfinn Karlsefni had a stockade built around the small encampment in fear that the Skraelings would attack the colony. The next summer, the natives did return, and this time one was killed while trying to steal weapons from one of the colonists. The other natives left but soon returned with "a great multitude of Skraeling boats." The Vikings were attacked by the natives, and the natives were defeated. Thorfinn only spent one more winter there. Fearing that the Skraelings finally would kill all the colonists, he led them back to Greenland. The next encounter between Norsemen and natives came the summer before they left. The *Greenland Saga* gives us a description of that encounter:

> It was now that they made acquaintance with the Skraelings (their name for natives who were either American Indians or Eskimos), when a big body of men appeared out of the forest there. Their cattle were close by; the bull began to bellow and bawl his head off, which so frightened the Skraelings that they ran off with their packs, which were of grey furs and sables and skins of all kinds, and headed for Karlsefni's house, hoping to get inside there, but Karlsefni had the doors guarded. Neither party could understand the other's language. Then the Skraelings unslung their bales, untied them, and proffered their wares, and above all wanted weapons in exchange. Karlsefni, though, forbade them the sale of weapons. And now he hit on this idea; he told the women to carry out milk to them, and the moment they saw the milk that was the one thing they wanted to buy, nothing else. So that was what came of the Skraelings' trading; they carried away what they bought in their bellies, while Karlsefni and his comrades kept their bales and their furs.[3]

An interesting final story about Thorfinn Karlsefni is that he had a figurehead carved for his ship from the maple wood found in Vinland. After his colony failed, he returned to Norway. On his way back to Norway, he stopped in Bremen and sold the figurehead, thus making the carved figurehead the first import to have come from North America to Europe.

The final early Viking voyage to Vinland of which there is a record was one of high adventure and intrigue. It was led by Freydis, the daughter of Erik the Red

3. Gwyn Jones, the *Greenland Saga*. In *The Norse Atlantic Sagas*, 156.

Who Were the Skraelings?

In the language spoken by the Vikings, *skraeling* was a term of contempt meaning "barbarian." It has long been debated among anthropologists who these people were. The argument centers on whether they were Eskimos or Algonquian Indians. Scientists have established that Eskimos lived along the coasts of Labrador and Newfoundland in the late ninth and early tenth centuries, while the Algonquian people lived farther west and south. But the Algonquians were far-ranging in their travel and likely visited the coast of Newfoundland from time to time. The Vikings called the Eskimos of Greenland "skraelings," but it was a generic term for native peoples they encountered everywhere in the North Atlantic region. The argument in favor of these "skraelings" being Algonquians relies on the physical descriptions presented in the sagas as well as the weapons used against the Vikings by these people. The encounter with native people found them using catapults (instruments that toss projectiles at the enemy) and bombards (animal stomachs filled with rocks or other materials and expanded with air so that they would explode on impact). Neither of these was used by Eskimos, but they were standard weapons of the Algonquians.

and sister of Leif Eriksson. She entered into partnership with two men from Iceland. The purpose of the trip seems to have been a commercial enterprise to cut timber to sell. Bad feelings between the Icelanders and the Greenlanders began as they settled in for the winter at Leifsbudir. Freydis wanted the Icelanders' ship, so she tricked her husband into believing that the Icelanders had molested her. He and the other Greenlanders killed the Icelanders while Freydis personally killed their five women. Freydis then took both ships and all the lumber back to Greenland to sell for her own profit.

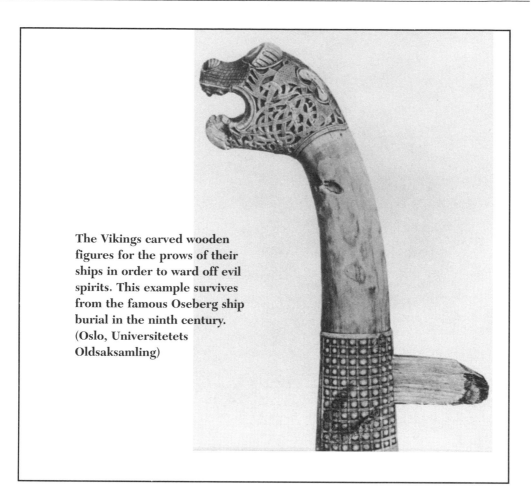

The Vikings carved wooden figures for the prows of their ships in order to ward off evil spirits. This example survives from the famous Oseberg ship burial in the ninth century. (Oslo, Universitetets Oldsaksamling)

There were no more attempts to colonize the lands to the west of Greenland after the Thorfinn Karlsefni effort. Scattered reports of a few more trips by Vikings to the west are registered in annals and chronicles. For example, a missionary bishop may have gone to Vinland in the early twelfth century, and a Greenland ship is recorded sailing for Markland in 1347. Even the Greenland settlement died out, and no more supply ships went there from Norway after 1410. It was not until the late sixteenth century that other Europeans began to learn of this early Viking activity in the North Atlantic.

The Vinland Map

On the facing page is the so-called Vinland Map, and it may be a fake. Even the best of scholars can be confused by historical documents from time to time, causing lasting controversy about a manuscript. This map surfaced in 1957 in Barcelona, Spain, and was eventually purchased in 1959 by an anonymous benefactor who gave it to Yale University. It is a map of Europe, but it generated a great deal of excitement because it showed an area southwest of Greenland labeled "the Island of Vinland, discovered by Bjarni and Leif in company." A longer text describes a visit to "Vinland" by a Bishop Erik in 1117-1118. In 1959 the Viking site at L'Anse aux Meadows had not yet been discovered, so to Viking enthusiasts this seemed the first real hard evidence of the Viking presence in the New World. Scholarly conferences were held and many newspapers and television and magazine reports told the public about the map. Despite all the publicity and passion aroused by the map, some scholars were skeptical because the map did not fit into what was known of European cartography. Especially disturbing to many was that Greenland seemed too perfectly drawn for the supposed date of the map. In 1967, the map was exhibited in several European cities and again questions were raised about its authenticity. Finally, in an effort to resolve all doubts, Yale University hired experts to make an investigation using the latest scientific equipment. Chemical tests were done in 1974 on the ink used to produce the map, and the tests showed that the map was a forgery. Microscopic anaylsis showed that the ink contained traces of titanium dioxide, which was not available commercially until after 1920. Nevertheless, some scholars continued to believe the map to be legitimate, regardless of evidence to the contrary. Because of the ongoing debate, another series of tests were ordered ten years later using a cyclotron to fire a beam of protons through the map. From this procedure, all elements in the ink and parchment could be identified and quantified. This time, the titanium amounts were shown to be only a trace and consistent with titanium's natural occurance in nature. When the Vinland map ink was compared to other medieval manuscripts, its titanium content was normal. In 1995, the issue of whether or not the map is a forgery was debated before a scholarly audience with the conclusion being in favor of its authenticity. This does not mean that everyone agreed to the Vinland map being genuine. The debate continues.

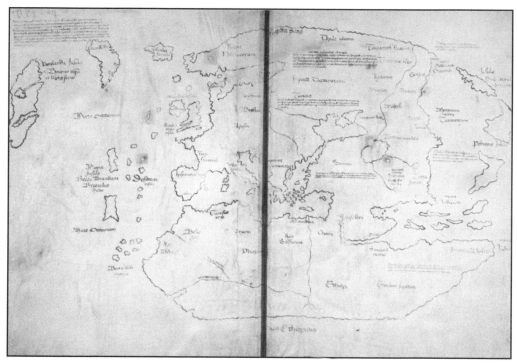

The Vinland Map (Yale University)

Sea Monsters and Land Animals

Note the sea monsters and animals that supposedly inhabited the northern Ocean Sea as drawn by Sebastian Munster in his book *Cosmographia* (Basel, 1550). In Munster's book he described each of the creatures. For example, the huge fish in the upper left and lower right corners were described to be as large as a mountain and found near Iceland (they were probably whales). Munster explained that they would overturn ships unless scared away by blowing trumpets. Another way to get rid of them was to throw barrels into the water because the fish loved to play with them. The large crustacean, center left, Munster stated would grab and kill a swimmer in its claws. The animals at the top of the drawing were both real and imagined. One can see reindeer, a lynx, and elks. The animal in the center of the picture, however, squeezed between two trees, was a creature who was so gluttonous that it would eat until full, squeeze itself between two trees causing it to vomit, and then rush back to eat some more. Munster stated that the best time to kill it was while it was caught between the trees. Its hide and fur were very valuable.

II.

JOHN CABOT AND THE REDISCOVERY
OF NORTH AMERICA

It would be nearly five hundred years after the Vikings' voyages before Europeans would again explore the shores of North America. By then, the adventures of the Vikings had been forgotten. During the late Middle Ages, Europeans began to expand their world in every respect: politically, scientifically, religiously, economically, and geographically. The geographic-economic expansion led to increased contact with Asia, especially China, where European travelers journeyed overland in increasing numbers. These travelers brought back tales of fabulous wealth that stimulated the imagination of European traders and merchants. Especially desirable were spices, which do not grow in Europe. Spices added flavor to foods, which were usually otherwise drab and poorly preserved. Additionally, some spices were seen to have medicinal properties needed to fight disease.

Geography in the Fifteenth Century

By the fifteenth century, geography was a topic of debate in the universities and among mapmakers, whose number included many sea captains and ship's pilots. No one questioned the shape of the earth, as can be seen by Martin Behaim's globe below. But the unknown parts of the world had to be envisioned before they could be explored, and that is what Behaim did on this part of his globe showing the Atlantic Ocean. For centuries, the Atlantic (or Ocean Sea as they called it then) had been described as the "Sea of Darkness" because myth and legend held dire tales about what was in that body of water. Human imagination pictured sea monsters, deformed and ferocious beings living on mythical islands, mermaids, giant whirlpools, and the like. People believed that there were hundreds, maybe thousands of islands in the Ocean Sea between Europe and Asia, but no one suspected the huge continental landmass of North and South America. It was thought that the Ocean Sea stretched from Europe to Asia across the back side of the globe.

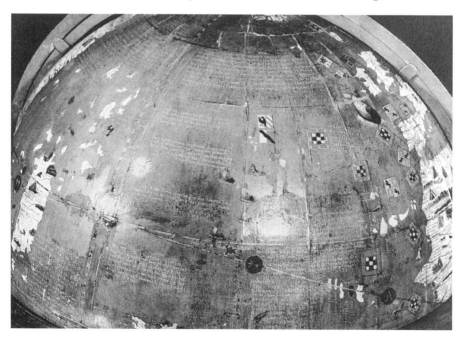

By the fifteenth century, overland transportation of goods to and from Asia had become extremely expensive, especially after the rise of the Ottoman Empire whose merchants controlled trade with the Far East and raised the price of commodities. Another problem was a diplomatic one. The Atlantic seaboard countries (for example, Spain, Portugal, England) were excluded from many Far Eastern markets by both the Near Easterners (such as the Ottoman Turks) and other European countries who already traded with them. Thus, an alternative route to the riches of the East became a high priority for Atlantic seaboard countries.

Portugal was the first to find another route to Asia by discovering a southern sea lane in 1488 around the tip of Africa and on to India. Spain followed shortly with the voyages of Columbus, who attempted to reach Asia by sailing west across the Ocean Sea. England followed next by authorizing the voyages of John Cabot, who believed that a still shorter route lay to the north in the Ocean Sea.

Sixteenth-century woodcut of Christopher Columbus by Tobias Stimmer (P. Jovius, *Elogia virorum bellica virtute illustrium*, Basle, 1575)

Christopher Columbus

The first European of record to land on the shores of the Americas was Christopher Columbus in 1492. Columbus was an Italian sea captain from Genoa sailing in the service of Spain in an attempt to find a route across the Ocean Sea to Asia. His life and efforts are well documented, and hundreds of biographies have been written about him. He left ships' logs of his trips, and letters, memoranda, and notes in the margins of the books he owned and the two books he wrote. Others who knew him also left records, including his son Ferdinand; and the governments for whom he worked left archives of his activities. After spending several years as a merchant sea captain carrying goods between the near ocean islands such as the Canaries, the Madeiras, and others, Columbus gave up a good living to follow his dream of crossing the Ocean Sea. He first sought support in Portugal and was turned down. Then he petitioned the monarchs of Spain, who finally authorized his voyage in 1492. Sailing with three ships, Columbus crossed the ocean from the Canary Islands to the Bahama Islands, and then he spent several weeks sailing among the islands of the Caribbean Sea. He was convinced that he was surrounded by islands off the coast of Asia. On his second voyage, he established the first colony in the New World on the north coast of Hispaniola (present-day Dominican Republic and Haiti). The third voyage took him farther south, where he discovered the South American continent. The last voyage was an attempt to find a passage around the lands he had found. He spent the trip sailing along the coast of Central America looking for a way through to Asia. Columbus never saw, nor landed, in North America.

Neither the Spanish nor the English adventurers accomplished their objective, but each established contact with the hitherto unknown continental landmass known today as North and South America. Contact soon deteriorated into conflict. European ships transported more than men and goods: they also carried European culture, values, religion, and diseases. Since the Western Hemisphere presented a barrier to the riches of the Orient, European countries eventually turned to exploiting the new lands they encountered. In the South, the Spanish and the Portuguese searched for gold and pearls, while in the North, the English and the French (and later the Dutch) searched for new sources of fish and fur.

Just as the first European encounter with North America had involved a father and son, Herjolf and Bjarni Herjolfsson, so too the European rediscovery and exploration of those same coasts would center on another father, John Cabot, and his son, Sebastian Cabot. John and Sebastian Cabot would sail there in the service of England. Surprisingly, we know even less about John Cabot than we do about the Vikings, and our information about Sebastian Cabot is untrustworthy. Thus, historians have had to dig into the archives to find the very few documents about the Cabots and deduce from these records the story of European rediscovery of North America. Consequently, several conflicting interpretations about the Cabots and their activities have arisen over the years. The important thing is that the Cabot voyages led to continued contact, whereas the Viking efforts had been nearly forgotten.

John Cabot was an Italian merchant seaman much like Christopher Columbus. His Italian name was Giovanni Caboto Montecatluña. A letter to the Spanish sovereigns, dated July 25, 1498, proclaims John Cabot to have been born in Genoa, Italy. Archives in Naples, Italy, and Valencia, Spain, seem to support this, but some scholars have made a good case that he was born in Catalonia, Spain. Records in the state archives of Venice show that sometime around 1461 Giovanni Caboto had moved to that city, and he became a naturalized citizen of

The Historical Sources for John and Sebastian Cabot

Unlike Christopher Columbus, John Cabot left us no documents. We have no letters, no ships' logs, no maps, nothing! Thus, the historian has to rely on scraps of information in an effort to reconstruct Cabot's life and accomplishments. One of the most exciting modern discoveries concerning him came in 1956, when the letter of an Englishman named John Day addressed to "the great admiral" was found. Scholars have assumed, based on the information surrounding the document, that "the great admiral" was Columbus, and that the letter was sent to Christopher Columbus to inform him about Cabot's voyages and discoveries. The letter was found in the General Archives of the city of Simancas in Spain. In the late fifteenth century, few records were kept of anyone unless he or she was of the highest nobility. A common coasting ship captain like John Cabot was not considered important enough to document in many records. He was of humble origins, and he died an untimely death. We can learn bits and pieces of information from the city records of Venice, Italy, where he became a naturalized citizen, and there are casual references to him in letters written by other people. There is no mention of him in England before 1495, and no one reports about him after 1498. The patents and payment receipts Cabot was given by King Henry VII survive in the Public Record Office of England, but these are most important for helping us to understand the king's attitude toward voyages of exploration. Besides the John Day letter, there are important letters written by Italian and Spanish diplomats who were at Henry VII's and Henry VIII's courts. A part of their job was to report economic activities to their home government. Voyages of exploration fell into this category.

The sources for Sebastian Cabot, his son, are both reliable and unreliable. Sebastian's world map of 1544, for example, credits both himself and his father for the 1497 voyage (which Sebastian mislabeled as having taken place in 1495). There are documents in the Public Record Office of England similar to those of his father's: letters, patent payments, etc. But Sebastian was a much more important person than his father because of his position as pilot major of Spain. The first historian of the exploration of the New World, Peter Martyr, knew Sebastian personally and interviewed him. In Peter Martyr's *De Orbe Novo Decades* lengthy paragraphs describe Sebastian's voyages but say nothing about his father. In fact, Martyr records things John Cabot did and credits them to Sebastian. The reason for this is probably that Sebastian claimed his father's achievements. There are also numerous letters written by prominent people in England, Spain, and Italy which tell about Sebastian and his various voyages. There are no portraits of John Cabot, but there is one of his son Sebastian. With such a lack of source material, scholars have debated almost every aspect of John and Sebastian Cabot's lives and accomplishments. Those debates continue to be very lively, and until other documents are found, many questions concerning the early rediscoverers of North America will not be resolved. This is why you will find this book often using words such as "maybe," "perhaps," and "it is believed."

Venice in 1476. In the early 1480s he married a lady named Mattea, and by 1484, the archives in Venice show that they had a family of sons named Lewis, Sebastian, and Sancio. These same sons are listed again years later (1496) in letters patent granted to John Cabot and his sons by the king of England. According to Sebastian Cabot, his father moved the family to England in 1485. The archives of Valencia, Spain, however, show that John Cabot was in that city in 1490, when he presented plans to improve that city's harbor. We know that he was in Spain when Christopher Columbus returned from his first voyage across the Ocean Sea in 1493. No one knows whether he ever met Columbus. He seems to have realized, however, that Columbus had not reached Asia as he planned. This encouraged Cabot to try. He was in Seville and Lisbon during 1493 or 1494 seeking backing for an ocean voyage of his own across the Ocean Sea. John Cabot had a good idea. He thought that the distance to Asia would be shortened sailing at northern latitudes, where the circumference of the earth is much smaller.

Cabot was a ship's captain who carried trading goods along the shores of the Mediterranean Sea. These coasting merchants were international traders. They had no strong attachments to their homelands and viewed all countries as places for personal profit. A merchant like John Cabot, or Christopher Columbus for that matter, acted as a middleman in European trade, taking goods from one country to another. They were on the lookout for new markets and new trade routes. Cabot was excited by the prospect of crossing the Ocean Sea after hearing of Columbus's success.

Seeking support and investors in Spain and Portugal, however, proved fruitless. Christopher Columbus had already tied up the Spanish backing, and the Portuguese were bound by the new Treaty of Tordesillas (1494), which established agreements to divide up discoveries west of Europe between Spain and Portugal. The Portuguese agreed not to explore beyond 1,175 miles west of Europe, and the Spanish agreed to stay out of Portugal's territory in the eastern Ocean Sea. This division was drawn on early maps and became known as the Line of Demarcation. Because of this treaty, John Cabot had little choice but to turn to England, which also was searching for new markets.

English coastal cities had long had an interest in the western ocean. The city of Bristol on the western coast of England and geographically midway between Iberia, as the Spanish peninsula is called, and Iceland was England's second largest seaport by the early fifteenth century. It owed its prosperity to its location. Bristol exported goods from the interior of England (for example, wool and woolen goods), collected cod from the sea near Iceland for import and export, and imported products from Iberia, especially wine and olive oil. Thus, in 1494, Bristolmen were very interested in the western Ocean Sea and were already fishing far to the west of Iceland. John Cabot, who was familiar with English seafaring, left Portugal for Bristol in 1494 or 1495. He soon made a number of important friends there, where his experience as a sea captain was known and respected. In a letter to the duke of Milan dated December 18, 1497, we are told that Cabot was "a foreigner and a poor man, [who] would not have obtained credence had it not been that his companions, who are practically all English and from Bristol, testified that he spoke the truth." This letter describes King Henry VII's visit to Bristol in 1496 and John Cabot's petition to the king for permission

to outfit an expedition to cross the Ocean Sea. Cabot was encouraged by the king to come to London and formally petition for that privilege. England had not been part of the Treaty of Tordesillas, which divided the New World between Spain and Portugal, so King Henry VII felt no need to obey it.

Portrait of King Henry VII, the first Tudor monarch. It was King Henry VII who sponsored John Cabot's first voyage. (National Maritime Museum, Greenwich)

Bristol Fishermen

The John Day letter, which is one of our best sources for the voyages of John Cabot, mentions that sailors from Bristol, England, had already sailed beyond Ireland to the "Isle of Brazil," one of the mythical islands everyone believed to exist in the Ocean Sea. Other evidence seems to indicate that Bristol seamen may have sighted the North American continent sometime in 1480 or 1481. The question remains, Why did they not tell anyone about this find? If it did happen, and it seems highly likely, the discovery was wrapped in secrecy for commercial reasons. Bristol seamen made a handsome living from fishing. The sighting of a "New Found Island" could have been made as they fished farther and farther across the northern Atlantic, finally reaching the Grand Banks off Newfoundland around this time. The Grand Banks are one of the best fishing grounds in the world, and no fisherman lets others know about his good fishing hole! In any case, the island spotted may have been Newfoundland or Nova Scotia. The fishermen may have then used this as a primary landmark to locate the fishing site. The Bristol fishermen kept the area secret as long as they could, and history proved that they were right to do so. By the sixteenth century, the Grand Banks saw a flood of fishermen from every maritime country in Europe, with hundreds of ships netting its waters. Scholars have long thought that both Columbus and Cabot knew about these early discoveries by men from Bristol, which encouraged each on his journey across the Ocean Sea. An interesting side note to the Grand Banks is that it is still one of the most popular commercial fishing areas in the world. Unfortunately, the unregulated fishing of the past five hundred years has left the area dangerously close to depletion of its fish and other marine life.

John Cabot was invited to Westminster to explain his plans to the king, and he easily sold the monarch on the prospect of opening the Asian trade to England by finding a new route to China across the North Atlantic. After listening to the Italian sea captain describe the wealth of Asia, the silks and spices, the gold and jewels and other riches, Henry VII issued a patent (a legal description defining what was to be accomplished and what was given as reward) authorizing Cabot to sail across the North Atlantic under the flag of England.

The patent named John Cabot, his heirs or deputies as successors, in the patent rights. Exploration was to be limited to the North Atlantic in order to avoid conflict with the Spanish in the South. Only lands of "heathens or infidels" could be seized, and if new trade was established with new lands, King Henry would receive one-fifth of the net profits. John Cabot was granted a monopoly over trade, with his sea route protected from competitors, or as the patent said, lands he discovered "may not be visited by any other subject of [England] without the license of John and his sons and of their deputies on pain of the loss of their ships and goods." Additionally, John Cabot was allowed to outfit up to five ships with the best provisions, but the costs must come from Cabot and his investors, not from the Crown. Henry VII would let Cabot take all the risks, physically and financially, while the Crown reaped the largest reward.

Now the record becomes dim again as to what happened next. John Cabot was back in Bristol before May 1496 and had selected the ship, *Mathew of Bristol*, for his voyage of discovery. We do not have the names of his investors, but without them he could not have leased the *Mathew*, supplied her, hired a crew, and planned his voyage.

The date of John Cabot's first attempt to cross the ocean is controversial. Most agree that it was around early May 1496. With a crew of twenty men, he set sail at high tide down the Avon River and on out to sea. This was the worst of times to attempt an ocean crossing. Strong winds were blowing in the wrong direction and each day he and his crew, sailing against the wind, lost time. The trip was a failure. After days of beating against the winds, and growing short on food and water, Cabot turned back. He had probably spent a great deal of his own money on outfitting the *Mathew*, which is why he was described as a "poor man" in the letter to the duke of Milan.

Legends of Early European Voyages to the West

There are many legends of ancient and medieval sailors who sailed out into the Ocean Sea. Ancient people such as the Phoenicians and Carthaginians sailed beyond the Pillars of Hercules at the entrance to the Mediterranian from 1100 B.C. onward, establishing colonies along the coasts of Europe and Africa. Irish monks especially wished to get away from civilization and tended to live on remote islands off the shores of their country. The most compelling legend, however, is of the sixth-century monk St. Brendan related in the first chapter.

In the early twelfth century, legend has it, a prince named Madoc from Wales, in western Britain, sailed across the Ocean Sea to another continent, but there is no proof of this.

The Canary Islands were found in the fifth century B.C. and settled by King Juba II of Numidia in North Africa around 25 B.C., but knowledge of the islands was lost and the colonists were left to develop their own culture. In the thirteenth century they were rediscovered by a ship blown off course, and in 1402 the Normans partly conquered them.

An Arab account written in the tenth century tells of a party of men from Cordova,

Spain, who sailed into the Ocean Sea and returned after several months with ships loaded with booty. Where did they go? No one knows.

Another Arab account relates an attempted ocean crossing around 1147 by eighty men called the "intrepid explorers." About three weeks after leaving Lisbon, they came to islands which could have been the Azores.

In 1291 two brothers from Genoa, Italy, Ugolino and Vadino Vivaldi, tried to cross the Ocean Sea to China and were never heard from again. In the fourteenth century two Venetians, Niccolo and Antonio Zeno, were rumored to have attempted the crossing and found an island in the western ocean.

Pre-Columbian contact in the Americas, other than that by the Vikings, remains unproven, but legends persist of ships blown off course, European coins found in the Western Hemisphere, and strangely carved or inscribed stones. The most visible result of all these legends and myths was a firm belief that certain islands existed in the Ocean Sea. Islands such as Brazil, Antilles, St. Brendan's, and the Green Isle continued to be placed on maps until the modern era.

Many people believed, for example, that the Island of the Seven Cities, or Antillia, was an occupied land far out in the Ocean Sea. According to the story, an archbishop and six bishops led refugees from the eighth-century Moorish invasion of Spain to new lands in the Ocean Sea named Antillia. Here each founded a city and the land was renamed the Land of the Seven Cities. It was believed that their descendants still lived there in perfect Christian communities that had become very rich from the gold found in Antillia. Since the Island was never found by early explorers, its location kept moving west until it was believed to be located in what is now the southwestern U.S. The Spaniard Coronado went looking for the Seven Cities in 1551, traveling through modern-day Arizona and exploring as far north as modern-day Kansas.

The next spring (1497), John Cabot began preparing for another attempt to cross the northern Ocean Sea. This time he left at the end of May with a crew of eighteen to twenty men (the sources vary). The winds were right and the *Mathew of Bristol* headed down the Avon River, out to sea, past Dursey Head (southwest coast of Ireland), and then on a straight route toward the New World. We have little information about the crossing except that a heavy storm was encountered at one point. On June 24, 1497, land was sighted off the coast of what is now Canada, probably somewhere between Cape Baud and Cape Bonavista, Newfoundland. It used to be thought that Cabot landed farther south at Cape Breton, but more recent research points to the location farther north. It would have been difficult for Cabot to have missed Newfoundland altogether, or to have ignored it and sailed on to Cape Breton. To the north, Cabot saw a large island, which he named St. John the Baptist. If the landfall was Cape Baud, then this island would be the one the French later called Belle Isle. Cape Baud is exactly across from Dursey Head. We know that Cabot tried to keep on a direct course at fifty-one degrees and thirty-three minutes. Both Cape Baud and Dursey Head are at that latitude. Thus, John Cabot probably landed not too far from the Viking camp at L'Anse aux Meadows. Perhaps more important to later voyages was that at whichever location it was, John Cabot and those with him were at the entrance of the St. Lawrence River of Canada. The topography and geography of the place convinced him that this was a transcontinental waterway, the famous Northwest Passage to Asia. From Cabot's first voyage on, men searched for the Northwest Passage which he, and later his son, claimed to be there.

The John Day letter is the most detailed about Cabot's activities in the New World. He coasted what is now Canada (maybe as far south as Maine in the United States) for a month or more and landed only once to take on fresh water. We do not know for sure where this landing was, but recent theory places it in Canada Bay.

Late fifteenth-century English ships as drawn in the Hastings Manuscript (Pierpont Morgan Library)

Ships in the Fifteenth Century

Just as we know very little about the ships taken by Columbus, the *Santa Maria*, the *Niña*, and the *Pinta*, we know even less about the ships used in northern ocean voyages.

The Spanish and Portuguese used the caravel, a light, low-in-the-water, rapid vessel adopted from the Muslims. The English adapted cargo vessels for extended ocean voyages. Coastal cargo ships, known as carracks, were longer and narrower and higher out of the water than caravals. They were not as fast nor as maneuverable, but they got the job done. The *Mathew* was what they called a "navicula" (meaning "little ship"). It probably had a large center mast with square sails, a foremast with a small square sail, and a lateen-rigged (triangle) mizzenmast. A navicula was between fifty and sixty feet long and had two decks. The *Mathew* was around fifty tons in size. Tonnage did not mean weight. Instead, tonnage (or tunnage) meant how many tuns, barrels used to carry wine, could be carried in a ship's cargo hold. By 1500, however, more and more ships were being built with two masts with square sails and a lateen mizzenmast. Such ships with this new rigging were more stable and faster than the *Mathew*.

Since these were basically commercial ships, they did not carry arms. At best they might have a small cannon used for communication (that is to contact another nearby ship by shooting a round to alert it), and maybe a few swords and pikes for sailors to use for fighting. Cannons used gunpowder, which was difficult to keep dry at sea; and when it was dry, it was a constant danger, for it could explode and blow up the ship. The most fearsome weapon in the late fifteenth century, and some were taken occasionally on ocean voyages, was the crossbow. John Cabot took at least one crossbow aboard the *Mathew*.

Suggested model of the *Mathew*. (Bristol Art Gallery)

While ashore, Cabot and his men planted the flags of England and Venice and a cross. No contact was made with local inhabitants although the crew noticed abandoned campfires and artifacts that showed human existence at the site. Cabot and others made a short walk through the woods, which is recorded by John Day in his letter to Columbus:

> They found big trees from which masts of ships are made, and other trees underneath them, and the land was very rich in pasturage, in which place they found a very narrow way leading into the land, and saw a spot where someone had made a fire. . . .[1]

1. John Day to the Lord Grand Admiral, in *The Cabot Voyages and Bristol Discovery under Henry VII*, ed. J. A. Williamson (Cambridge: Cambridge University Press, 1961), 212.

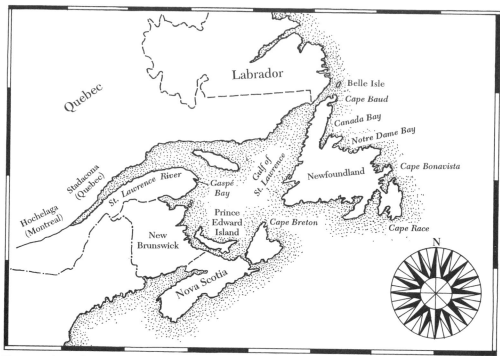

Eastern Canada

Boarding their ships, they continued on south, passing two large islands, to about forty-five degrees latitude according to John Day. Impressed by the large schools of fish, mostly cod and flounder, the crew caught, dried, and salted enough fish to fill the cargo hold of the *Mathew*.

Running low on provisions, John Cabot now returned north to the location of his first landfall, and then proceeded due east back across the ocean to England. The trip had taken thirty-five days from England to Newfoundland but only fifteen days to return because of a strong stern wind. Navigational confusion and debate between Cabot and his crew caused them to sail too far south on the return, landing them near Brittany in the north of France. Several days later, Cabot and his crew sailed into Bristol, arriving there on August 6.

After selling their cargo of "stockfish" in Bristol, John Cabot and his backers set out for London, reaching Westminster Palace on August 10, 1497. Everyone at court, including foreign diplomats, listened to their tales of adventure across the Ocean Sea. They displayed some of the artifacts found when they were on land, and Cabot had made a map and a globe to show the king where he had been. Unfortunately, that map and globe have disappeared.

King Henry VII was pleased, and promised a larger fleet for a return trip and rewarded Cabot with money from the royal treasury. Cabot spent the next weeks as a celebrity, as described in a letter from a Venetian in London to his brothers at home: "He is called the Great Admiral and great honor is paid to him, and he goes dressed in silk, and these English run after him like [they are] mad. . . ."[2] On August 23, Cabot returned to Bristol.

Both Christopher Columbus and John Cabot had the same goals: to find a sea route to Asia, establish trading agreements with the great Khan in China, and find the source of the spice trade. Both failed, but both firmly believed that they were near their objectives. Neither realized that they had encountered the continents of the Americas. Relying on the geographical information available in the fifteenth century, the combination of medieval and Renaissance cartography and travelers' stories as described in the last chapter, both believed that they were near their goals, and that they had reached islands off the coast of Asia. Christopher Columbus made four voyages searching for Asia; Cabot would try only one more time.

In another Venetian's letter, he writes that he talked to Cabot about his plans for a second voyage:

[Cabot] has his mind set upon even greater things, because he proposes to keep along the coast from the place at which he touched, more and more towards the east, until he reaches an island which he calls Cipangu [Japan] . . . where he believes all the spices of the world have their origins as well as jewels.[3]

2. Lorenzo Pasqualigo to his Brothers at Venice, in *Cabot Voyages*, 208.
3. Raimondo de Raimondi de Soncino to the Duke of Milan, in *Cabot Voyages*, 210.

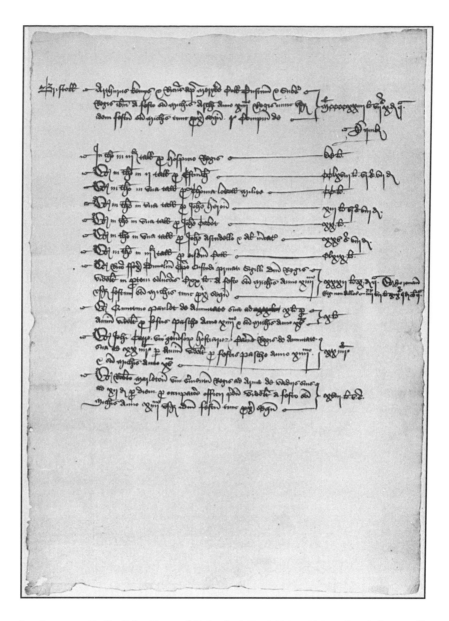

From the Customs Roll of the Port of Bristol, A.D. 1496–1499, "The Cabot Roll."
(British Library) This document shows authorization for a pension to John Cabot. The
fifth entry of the text reads: "In the treasury in three talleys in the name of the kings
household . . . John Cabot 20.00 (pounds)."

Cabot returned to London, where he spent the winter. King Henry VII granted him a pension, and on February 3, 1498, a new patent for discovery. This time the king gave him six ships, but only five ships were finally outfitted for the second voyage. King Henry this time promised an armed vessel, which the king leased from London merchants and pressed into service. The other four ships were from Bristol. The second voyage was opened to investors and colonists. In the second patent, King Henry had included that "[Cabot] may take and receive into the said ships . . . our subjects as of their own free will who would go . . . with him to the said land and islands."

There were perhaps around two hundred people who enlisted for the voyage. Some were farmers and craftsmen, and many were merchants who planned on trading goods they took aboard ship and then returning to England. A group of "poor friars" (either Franciscan or Dominican brothers, maybe both) signed up to accompany Cabot, who promised to make them all bishops in the new land.

The ships, their crews, and the passengers were ready by late April, 1498. Cabot and his fleet left Bristol at the beginning of May. After sailing westward beyond Dursey Head for several days, the fleet hit a heavy storm. The winds tore at the sails and riggings, and one ship began to take on water. It headed back to the coast of Ireland. The other four ships proceeded on the voyage and were never heard from again.

What happened to John Cabot and the remaining four ships is a complete mystery. They may have made it on through the storm and perished later in North America, or they may have been swallowed by the sea. The confusion arises because of an event a few years later. In 1501, a Portuguese expedition under Gaspar and Miguel Côrte Real encountered native peoples in Newfoundland wearing "silver rings which without doubt seem to have been made in Venice," and these same natives had in their possession "a piece of broken gilt sword" made in Italy. These artifacts of earlier contact between Europeans and Native

Life Aboard Ship

Ships were meant for carrying cargo, to produce a profit, and thus they had little comfort for those on board. Men slept where they could on deck, on a pile of rope, or curled up in a corner. One of the greatest gifts from the New World was the hammock, which sailors quickly adopted for a bed aboard ship. It could be put up at night and removed in the morning. Plus, it was comfortable!

For food, sailors had some dried and salted pork and beef, but the mainstay at sea was "hardtack," a biscuit made before leaving port, which always molded and got maggots in it before the voyage ended. The only fresh food was fish caught while sailing or wild game killed if they landed. Beer was the main drink, with hard cider on occasion. Water was precious and hard to keep, but it could be caught in sails and buckets during a storm. Everyone cooked his own food (when a fish was caught for example) on the "cook box," an iron stove located on a bed of sand aboard ship.

Each sailor supplied his own clothes. Most wore baggy trousers and a long shirt with a hood for cold weather.

Ships were filled with vermin—mice, lice, roaches, bugs, and sometimes rats. It was standard practice to take one or two cats along to keep the mice from multiplying. The bilgewater (water that collected under the bottom deck) was polluted and smelled bad. Sailors tended to throw garbage into the bilge too, which made it worse.

Going to the toilet meant being swung out over the ocean on a swing if the weather was good. If the weather was stormy, one went to the toilet wherever one could on the ship.

Seamen were tough and rough, but they were also religious. Proper religious services were held aboard ship, and it was part of the cabin boy's duty to call seamen to prayer and thanksgiving. After the Protestant Reformation in England, ships carried a copy of the Book of Common Prayer, which was read each morning and evening.

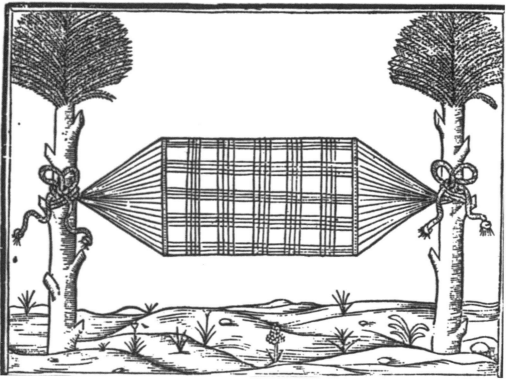

Early woodcut of New World hammock adopted by sailors from Europe

Americans have caused much speculation among historians. Were these items taken from Cabot on his ill-fated second voyage, or were they objects simply discarded or lost on the first voyage? No one will ever know unless modern archaeological investigation someday locates Cabot's ships from the second voyage off the shores of North America, or discovers an attempted colonial site built by these adventurers.

Uncertainty about the fate of Cabot's fleet did not cause immediate alarm in England. After all, Cabot had planned to be gone for several months searching for Asia and establishing a trading colony. Even as time passed, it was impossible for another fleet to sail, for the patent given to John Cabot was exclusive in its privileges. But the Portuguese did not feel constrained by an English patent.

Navigation

Navigation is simply the science of going somewhere and getting back. The Vikings had navigated the northern sea mostly by knowing its environment, recognizing currents and marine life, and by keeping the sun and stars in the right relationship to the ship. Furthermore, the Vikings, as noted in the first chapter, sailed on a route staying close to Iceland, Greenland, and Vinland. Sailors in the fifteenth century were able to sail the open ocean because navigational equipment had become more sophisticated. The compass, invented during the late Middle Ages, allowed pilots to know direction regardless of whether they could see the sun. Other instruments enabled pilots to approximate their position on the ocean by measuring the angle between the horizon and either the North Star or the sun, and then taking that data and applying it to sets of tables already worked out, which would show the mariner his degrees of latitude. The astrolabe, the cross-staff, and the quadrant each helped in these calculations, although all were difficult to use accurately aboard a rolling ship. Nevertheless, an experienced sailor could do it with some degree of precision. In order to measure speed at sea, crude systems were devised. Most experienced mariners, however, could "feel" the speed of a ship to a close exactness. Ships used a sandglass which held one half hour of material to keep track of time. One of the most important jobs for a ship's boy was to turn the sandglass when the material inside fell to the bottom. Failure to do so led to severe punishment, for the sandglass was essential to many of the activities aboard ship, as well as to navigation.

John Cabot and the English explorations had caused alarm among both the Spanish and the Portuguese. They believed that they had carved out the rights to territories in the Ocean Sea for themselves through the Treaty of Tordesillas. Spain had been concerned when it learned that Cabot's second voyage was to sail

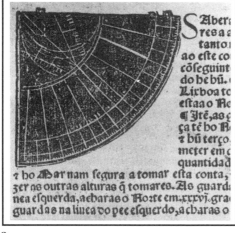

a.

b.

c.

a. A quadrant from *Reportório dos tempos* (Lisbon, 1563)

b. A cross-staff being used. From Pedro de Medina, *Regimiento de navegación* (Seville, 1563)

c. A mariner's astrolabe being used. From Pedro de Medina, *Regimiento de navegación* (Seville, 1563)

south looking for Cipangu. This is what brought on the correspondence between John Day and Christopher Columbus. It seemed as though Cabot was planning to sail into Spanish territory in the Caribbean Sea. The Portuguese were worried that Cabot's discoveries on the first voyage were within their sphere of influence.

Taking advantage of the Portuguese concerns, João Fernandes, a small landowner and mariner from the Azores island of Terceira, sought a patent for exploration from King Manuel I of Portugal in the fall of 1499. Some historians believe that Fernandes also may have had Bristol investors who supported him in order to discover the fate of John Cabot and his four ships. The Fernandes family had traded with Bristol merchants for several years and many people in Bristol knew João. Some scholars believe that João Fernandes may have even had relatives who had gone with Cabot on his second voyage. In any case, Fernandes was granted the Portuguese patent on October 28, 1499, which gave him exploration and trading privileges, but also left it up to him to find his own financial backing.

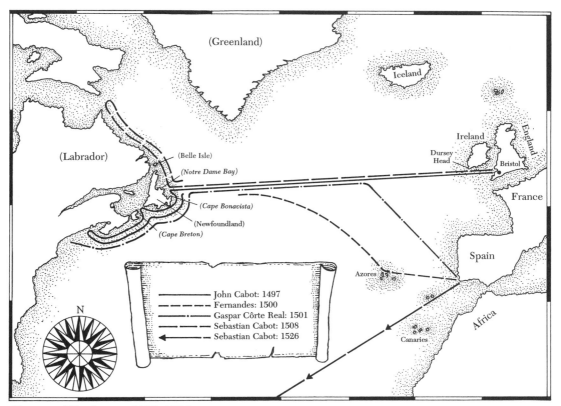

Routes of Explorers, 1497–1526

The Fernandes expedition left Lisbon in May 1500 heading first to the Azores and then due north, making a long arc toward Newfoundland. Unfortunately, Fernandes sailed into a sea of ice floes and icebergs near Greenland and had to turn back. Fernandes's failure voided his patent in Portugal, so he went to England in order to obtain a similar agreement from King Henry VII.

One of Fernandes's investors in 1499 had been Gaspar Côrte Real, another landowner and mariner from the island of Terceira in the Azores. He was also a cousin of King Manuel of Portugal. Now Gaspar Côrte Real applied for a Portuguese patent of discovery. It would appear from Gaspar Côrte Real's patent that he had information about John Cabot's discoveries of 1497. Starting from Lisbon in 1501, Côrte Real followed roughly the same track across the northern sea as Cabot and seems to have landed at approximately the same location in Newfoundland. This is where he found the natives with the European artifacts mentioned earlier. Historians have concluded that Côrte Real might have had sailing charts made by Cabot.

Cabot had only landed briefly and taken note of signs of native peoples (fireplaces, carved objects, and the like), but Gaspar Côrte Real explored the shores and inlets and encountered the native Beothuk people. He took sixty of them captive and planned to bring them back to Portugal as slaves.

Côrte Real continued exploring to the south, spending several days in Notre Dame Bay. Finally, he decided to send one of his ships home, probably commanded by his brother Miguel Côrte Real, along with seven native people. Gaspar Côrte Real continued coasting North America and disappeared forever.

Miguel Côrte Real returned to Portugal in early October 1501 and soon worried when his brother had not joined him. He petitioned the king for a patent to go look for his brother, which was granted, and he left for a new voyage in May 1502. Arriving at Notre Dame Bay, Miguel split up his fleet, sending each of his three ships in a different direction to search for his brother. They planned to

Description of the Beothuk People

We do not know very much about the Beothuk people who were the natives in that area of Newfoundland when John Cabot and others landed there. They were hunters and gatherers whose language may have been related to Algonquian. It has been estimated that when John Cabot landed in 1497 they numbered only about five hundred people. They are now gone completely. The Beothuk lived in small bands of a few related families, each with its own chief. Early explorers recorded that they were expert at maneuvering their small canoes, from which they speared seals and fished for salmon and shellfish. In the forest, they hunted game with bow and arrows. Since they smeared red ocher on their faces and bodies for religious reasons and to keep off insects, they were referred to as "Red Indians" by early Europeans, which is probably the origin of that designation for all northern native peoples.

regroup on August 20. Miguel never arrived at the designated meeting place. The other two ships waited for him a few days, gave up, and returned to Portugal. Miguel Côrte Real was lost too.

The disaster of the Côrte Real brothers caused Newfoundland to be called the Land of Côrtereal for a while. The Portuguese king stopped sending voyages there because it was too costly in lives and ships lost. As one writer of the day said:

There is little knowledge because the land is very cold and of little value, and the two brothers Côrte Real died there with all their men, although it is not known how, for nothing was ever heard of them from a short while after they reached that place; for which reason, and because of the small value of the land, the King of Portugal has not sought to send thither any more men or ships.[4]

Even so, the earlier reports of great quantities of salmon, herring, and cod would lure fishermen to the area for years to come. Portugal lost interest in finding a western route across the northern ocean to Asia because in 1499 Vasco da Gama, another Portuguese mariner and explorer, had finally sailed all the way around the tip of Africa and across the Indian Ocean to India. Portugal had achieved its goal in the southern seas.

The Côrte Reals were not the only Europeans exploring the coast of Newfoundland in 1501 and 1502; English expeditions organized by João Fernandes sailed again in both years. Fernandes had left Portugal for Bristol, England, after failing on his first attempt to cross the northern Atlantic. He quickly put together a partnership with Bristol merchants and together they petitioned King Henry VII for a patent for exploration. In March 1501 the patent was issued allowing them to "recover, discover, and search out whatsoever islands, countries, regions or provinces of heathens and infidels in whatsoever part of the world they may lie, which before this time were unknown to all Christians." The patent gave the partners a ten-year monopoly on all they discovered, with King Henry receiving a healthy 20 percent.

There are almost no details about the Fernandes voyage of 1501 other than that it went to Newfoundland and returned. Encouraged, another trip was made in 1502, but little is known about it either. Sources record that an eagle was brought back by one of the seamen, for which the king rewarded him, and that three Beothuk natives were presented to the court. It is evident that King Henry

4. Alonso de Santa Cruz on the North-Western Discoveries, in *Cabot Voyages*, 232.

VII, like Manuel I of Portugal, was growing tired of the costs in terms of equipment and lives. In his patent of 1502 to Fernandes and his Bristol partners, King Henry stated that these voyages were full of "great costs and heavy charges . . . as well as dangers both to their persons and to their good and chattels . . . in such a difficult, tempestuous, dangerous and distant maritime undertaking."[5]

Word of the abundance of fish, however, caused other countries to enter the northern sea by sending fishing fleets to the Grand Banks off Newfoundland. Fish was a staple in the European diet, and catching and importing fish was a lucrative business. The Bretons, French, Basques, Portuguese, and other fishermen did not feel bound by any patent rights from foreign kings. Everyone soon discovered that the Grand Banks was one of the easiest and most profitable fishing grounds in the Atlantic.

Despite King Henry's growing concern about voyages of exploration, Englishmen did continue to sail to the New World in the early sixteenth century, and as usual, we have little information about their success. The most publicized voyages, however, would come with Sebastian Cabot, the son of John Cabot, who set out to continue his father's discoveries shortly after the death of King Henry VII.

Sebastian Cabot spent his early life in the port city of Bristol, England, where his father had settled. Here he heard the stories of Bristol seamen sailing out into the Ocean Sea, and he knew how his father had crossed that great body of water. Indeed, some people believe that Sebastian had been on the ill-fated voyage of 1498 and was one of those on the ship that turned back. As we have seen, he seems to have claimed credit for his father's voyages, and many early histories of discoveries ascribe them to him. Much of his adult life was spent in the service of Spain, but in his later years he returned to England, where he lived mostly in London, promoting English exploration and colonization across the northern Atlantic.

5. Letters Patent Granted to Hugh Elyuot, Thomas Asshehurst, João Gonsalves, and Francisco Fernandes, 9 December 1502, in *Cabot Voyages*, 259.

Portrait of Sebastian Cabot copied from lost original (Massachusetts Historical Society)

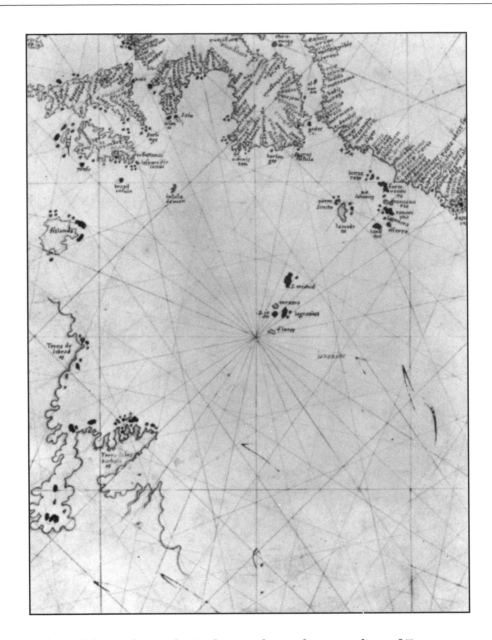

A chart of the northern Atlantic showing the northern coastlines of Europe, England, Iceland, Greenland, and Newfoundland from a portolan atlas made in 1508. A portolan map enables ships' pilots to find their way from point to point. (British Museum, London)

Sebastian Cabot had a desire to follow in his father's footsteps at a time when there seemed little left to discover. Sebastian claimed to have made a voyage in 1508, but the sources are contradictory about it. It would seem that he left England with two ships, probably paid for from his own funds, and sailed north looking for an Arctic passage to Asia. Encountering ice floes and icebergs somewhere off Labrador, he was forced by his crews, by some accounts, to turn south, which he did, and he continued coasting down North America. His lifelong insistence that he knew of a northern passage to Asia may indicate that he went far enough north to have seen the entry to Hudson Bay. How far south he went no one knows. Estimates run all the way from Chesapeake Bay to Florida. He mentions meeting native peoples along the trip south and that they were highly intelligent. He returned to England to find that Henry VII had died and that Henry VIII was now king. Henry VIII and his counselors were not much interested in new voyages of discovery.

Shortly after this we find Sebastian Cabot was living in London again, where he married a woman named Joanna in 1509. They had a daughter whom they named Elizabeth. Sebastian had two things that enabled him to pursue his dreams: his father's reputation and his own abilities as a cartographer.

England and France went to war in 1511, and Sebastian was recruited as a mapmaker by the English forces. Spain was England's ally in this war, which gave Sebastian Cabot an opportunity to meet with Spanish officials to discuss a possible ocean voyage. He showed them maps he had made of the Ocean Sea, told them about his father's voyages, and said that he had gone to the New World in 1508. A deal was worked out between the English and Spanish governments for Sebastian to go to Spain and work. Sebastian was granted leave from his duties for the English at the request of King Ferdinand of Spain and moved to Spain, where he was employed as one of the pilots of the Casa de Contratación. The Casa de Contratación, located at Seville, was the headquarters for the Spanish exploration and colonization activities in the New World. The Casa de Contratación was also an institute for licensing, controlling, and teaching all aspects of navigation. Sebastian was hopeful that when the war ended, he would be funded for his own voyage to the New World, where he planned to find a passage through the newly found lands, westward to Asia. But fate did not cooperate. Sebastian's patron, King Ferdinand, died in 1516, to be succeeded by King Charles.

Sebastian ultimately was promoted to pilot major of Spain, but funding for a trip of discovery was not forthcoming from the new king. The main job of the pilot major was to keep the official maps of Spain up to date. In 1519, Sebastian went back to England to petition King Henry VIII to fund a voyage for him. In the petition to the king, Sebastian seems to have asserted that he, Sebastian, and not his father, had made the earlier voyages of discovery. Henry VIII was interested and in March 1521 he requested that merchants and craft guilds in London and Bristol outfit ships at their own cost for Sebastian. The merchants and craft guilds protested about having to foot the bill. Not only did the leaders of these groups think that such a voyage was a waste of money, they did not trust nor believe Sebastian Cabot's claims of earlier voyages. In fact, they even doubted that he was qualified as a ship's captain. In their protest report to the king they said:

> We think it would . . . jeopardize five ships with men and goods . . . [to] trust the man called . . . Sebastian, which Sebastian as we here say was never in that land himself [New World], as all he makes reports of many things as he has heard his father and other men speak about in times past.[6]

The king was embarrassed! It looked as though he had backed a liar. He banished Sebastian Cabot from England forever. Sebastian returned to his position as pilot major of Spain.

6. The Plans for the Expedition of 1521, in *Cabot Voyages*, 287.

Sebastian now sought support from his father's place of citizenship, Venice, Italy. The merchants and city leaders considered his plans for a voyage of discovery to locate a passage through the New World to Asia, but in the end they rejected his project. It may have been during this time that Joanna, Sebastian's wife, died. He then married a Castilian lady named Doña Catalina Medrano.

Sebastian Cabot's fortune changed. King Charles reorganized the Casa de Contratación in 1524, giving it a new name, the Council of the Indies. In an effort to open Spanish trade to other nations, on September 2, 1524, the new officials of the Council of the Indies authorized Sebastian Cabot to organize an expedition of international merchants to search for a better passage across the Americas to Asia. Ferdinand Magellan had sailed around the world, but to do so he had had to go around the southern tip of South America, a very long journey. Sebastian, and earlier his father, believed that there was a waterway across the vast Western Hemisphere continents. The patent to sail of 1524, however, seems to have been for an attempt to locate a westward passage up the Rio de la Plata, Spanish territory in South America, not across North America.

Now things began to move for Sebastian. With a patent from the Spanish king, he would finally realize his dream of following in his father's footsteps. Four ships were commissioned for the voyage. The *Santa Maria de la Concepción* would be Sebastian's flagship, followed by the *Trinidad*, the *Santa Maria de L'Espinar*, and the *San Gabriel*. The ships were rented by merchants from England and Spain and the crews were of many nationalities—Spaniards, Italians, Germans, Greeks, and Portuguese, among others.

The fleet left Spain on April 3, 1526, and the trip lasted for four years. The fleet sailed to Brazil and headed south; bad weather sank the *Santa Maria de la Concepción*, Sebastian's flagship. Hearing about a mountain of pure silver up the Rio de la Plata, Sebastian ignored his orders to find a passage across South America, and instead he looked for the mountain. After many months searching for silver, he had found nothing, and several of his men had been killed by hunger, disease, and attacks by native people. Sebastian sailed back to Spain on the *Santa Maria de L'Espinar,* arriving in July, 1530. In order to show some profit to his investors, he had loaded the ship with native peoples to be sold as slaves.

Since he had disobeyed orders, and since many of those who had gone with him accused him of several crimes, Sebastian Cabot was forced to answer charges before a special judicial court. In 1531 he was found guilty of disobeying the king's orders, fined a large amount of money, and banished to Morocco. But Cabot appealed his case to King Charles, who was intrigued by the tales of a mountain of silver. The king reversed the sentence and reappointed Sebastian pilot major. He remained in Spain for the next seventeen years.

The failed expedition continued to plague Sebastian for the rest of his life. Many investors had lost money and many men had lost their lives. Eventually, Sebastian left Spain in 1547 to return to England. Young Edward VI was now king of England, and most of Sebastian's past had been forgotten by the English. Always promoting himself as a noted explorer, Sebastian began to seek another voyage to the New World. He cast his failed expedition of 1526 in the best light possible by telling of the silver that had distracted him from his goal to find a passage across the continent. He also claimed that he had begun the trip off the coast of Newfoundland in the north, and that he had found a Northwest Passage to Asia, which he placed on his famous map of 1544. He seems to have implied that his father had also noticed this Northwest Passage to Asia. With such tales he was able to interest important investors, who began to petition the king for him to authorize another voyage.

The trip never materialized. Young King Edward VI died and his sister, Mary, ascended the throne to begin years of religious turmoil in England. Eventually she was beheaded and succeeded by her sister, Elizabeth I. Sebastian Cabot lived out his days seeking new funding until he died in 1557. His greatest achievement was that he kept alive the English interest in the northern Atlantic and in the northeastern American continent. His belief that there was a northern passage through that continent would continue to inspire explorers for decades, but it would not be found until the twentieth century, when icebreakers finally made it through and nuclear submarines sailed under the ice cap covering the Arctic Ocean.

III.

THE FRENCH IN NORTH AMERICA

France was the last of the great European powers to sponsor transoceanic exploration activities in the early years of European discovery, because it had been involved in wars in Europe. Then three things seemed to have decided King Francis I to encourage ventures across the Atlantic: the return of Magellan's ship loaded with Asian spices in 1522, the capture of three Spanish ships laden with Spanish treasure from the New World by the French navy, and reports of Bretons about the rich Grand Banks fishing area off Newfoundland.

In 1523, Francis I commissioned an Italian sea captain by the name of Giovanni da Verrazano to sail to North America for the French in order to find a passage through the continent to the Orient and to assess the possibilities of trade with natives in North America. Giovanni da Verrazano was from a wealthy Florentine family with trading and banking ties in France. He was an expert navigator and sea captain. Thus, France too relied on Italian expertise, just as Spain had with Columbus, England had with Cabot, and Portugal had with Amerigo Vespucci.

Verrazano was not immediately successful. His fleet of four ships ran into a storm. Two of the ships sank and two ships, storm damaged, returned to port in Brittany. The two ships were repaired, but instead of being sent across the Ocean Sea again, Verrazano and the two ships were sent to Spain because France and Spain were at war. When he returned, however, Verrazano was again given orders to search for a route to the Orient through the North American mainland. Verrazano this time chose to sail from the Madeira Islands. He refitted his ship, the *Dauphine*, with the latest navigational instruments and provisions for eight months. On January 17, 1524, he sailed from the islands straight across the Atlantic, making landfall near what is today Cape Fear, North Carolina.

Giovanni da Verrazano (Pierpont Morgan Library)

Giovanni da Verrazano did not find a way through the North American land-mass, but he did add to the lore that such a passage existed. His major contribution to the history of exploration was that he systematically explored and recorded the features of the east coast of North America from Cape Fear to Newfoundland. His major error was to believe that the narrow Outer Banks Islands off North Carolina separated the Atlantic and Pacific Oceans. The Outer Banks Islands are a mile wide and nearly two hundred miles in length. He thought Pamlico Sound to the west of them was the Pacific.

Strangely, Verrazano missed the eleven-mile entrance to the Chesapeake Bay, but he was the first European to enter and describe New York Bay and the Hudson River. Thus, today, the great bridge that crosses from Brooklyn to Staten Island bears his name. Verrazano is also important to the anthropology and historical geography of North America. He frequently anchored the *Dauphine* to go on shore and investigate the things he saw, and he described the land and the many native American groups he encountered. In July, 1524, he returned to France.

Verrazano was a well-educated man, and he wrote a lengthy report of his adventures. This report made to King Francis I was circulated throughout France, providing natural scientific and ethnographical (that is, cultural data

This ship found on the Verrazano Map is probably the *Dauphine* (Vatican Library)

Verrazano's Description of One Group of Natives He Encountered

Giovanni da Verrazano's account of his trip is filled with ethnological information about the peoples he encountered. Here is one example of people living in the region between modern New York City and Newport, Rhode Island: "This is the most beautiful people and the most civilized in customs that we have found in this navigation. They excel us in size; they are of bronze color, some inclining more to whiteness, others to tawny color; the face sharply cut, the hair long and black, upon which they bestow the greatest study in adorning it; the eyes black and alert, the bearing kind and gentle. . . . Their women are of the same beauty and charm; very graceful; of comely mien and agreeable aspect; of habits and behavior as much according to womanly custom as pertains to human nature . . . the head bare, with various arrangements of braids, composed of their own hair, which hang on one side. . . . Some use other hair arrangements like the women of Egypt and of Syria use, and these are they who are advanced in age and are joined in wedlock. . . ."[1]

1. Verrazano Letter, 8 July 1524, in *The Discovery of North America*, ed. W. Cumming, R. Skelton, and D. Quinn (New York: American Heritage Press, 1971), 83.

about the people who lived there) information about the New World. Unfortunately, it also contained errors such as Verrazano's belief that only a narrow isthmus divided the Atlantic and Pacific Oceans. The theory that the waters between the Outer Banks and the mainland of North America were an arm of the Pacific offered new hope that a Northwest Passage to the Orient could be found. The "arm" of the Pacific came to be named "Verrazano's Sea."

Theodor de Bry woodcuts (Frankfort/Main, 1590) depicting North American natives in the area of the Virginias

France could do little with Verrazano's information about North America. Upon the explorer's return, the country suffered a series of disastrous military defeats, including one battle in which King Francis I was himself captured and held prisoner by the Spanish. Thus, French exploration activities were put on hold for the next decade. By the time Francis I was again ready to commission exploration activity, Giovanni da Verrazano was dead. He had been captured by Caribs off the coast of South America and eaten by them as his horrified crew watched.

An Early Tourist Cruise

Maybe the strangest tale from these times is the tourist cruise to the newfound lands organized by Richard Hore. Hore was a leather merchant of London who chartered two ships, the *Trinity* and the *William,* for the double purpose of codfishing and giving a group of English gentlemen a pleasure cruise. This first tourist cruise to North America ended in misery. The ships departed in late April 1536. Somewhere in the Atlantic the *Trinity* was lost. The *William,* however, continued on to Newfoundland. After two months, the provisions they had brought with them ran out and the tourists and crew had to live off the land, eating fish and osprey eggs. Then they resorted to eating raw plants and roots. When all resources ran out, they turned to cannibalism. Finally a French ship arrived, and the English who had survived the ordeal captured it for its food and to provide passage home. There would be no more tourist cruises to North America for the next two centuries.

It was almost a decade before the French government resumed exploration activities in North America. In the meantime, French fishermen were busy fishing in the rich Grand Banks off Newfoundland. Finally, in 1534, France renewed its exploration activities by financing the famous Jacques Cartier, an experienced mariner from Saint-Malo. This investment would ultimately reap great rewards for France.

As is the case with most of the northern explorers, little is known about the life of Jacques Cartier. He was born in Saint-Malo, France, in 1491, and at the age of twenty-eight he married the daughter of a government official. He is listed in the civic records as a "master pilot of the port of Saint-Malo." We have little idea how he achieved this status. There is no doubt about his navigational skills,

Jacques Cartier engraving done from portrait in Saint-Malo in *Histoire de la Nouvelle France*, Paris, 1744

however. Cartier probably started his career as a *mousse* (ship's boy) when he was around thirteen years old. He then would have risen through the ranks of novice and sailor. He must have had some experience sailing the North Atlantic or he would not have been commissioned to lead the French expedition of 1534. He hinted in one document that he may have already sailed to South America because he compared the corn growing in the St. Lawrence River region to that of Brazil. Jean le Veneur, the bishop of Saint-Malo, recommended him to the king and told the king that Captain Cartier had sailed to both Brazil and Newfoundland. When he was chosen to lead the French expedition, he was just over forty years old.

Cartier was commissioned by the king to take two ships to the "New Lands" to discover islands or countries from which gold or other valuables could be taken. But this was only the written agenda. From all Cartier's actions, it seems certain that the real purpose of his voyage was to find a way across the "New Lands" to Asia. Cartier left Saint-Malo on April 20, 1534, with two small ships and a crew of about sixty men. They sailed westward to Newfoundland, making landfall in just three weeks. Because of the ice pack near Newfoundland, Cartier was forced south without landing. Rounding the southern tip of Newfoundland, he turned north and explored the Gulf of St. Lawrence along the Labrador coast.

Finding nothing of interest along the Labrador coast, which was so barren that he described it as "the land that God allotted to Cain," Cartier sailed south to the western coast of Newfoundland and then west toward what is today Prince Edward Island. At Chaleur Bay he met several of the Micmac people, with whom he traded.

The farther inland Cartier went the better the land was, and he found wild berries, corn, birds, and animals. He continued on westward to Anticosti Island, from where he could see the shores of modern-day Quebec Province. This great bay looked like it might be the beginning of the passage to Asia, but local descriptions of the St. Lawrence River discouraged Cartier. At the northern entrance to the Gulf of St. Lawrence, he met large numbers of native peoples who were friendly and traded valuable furs with the French. They reported that the river narrowed farther inland toward the land of Canada (the native's name for the interior). Thus, Cartier reasoned that this was probably not a passage across the North American continent. By now it was August and the weather was beginning to change. Further exploration of the St. Lawrence would have to wait. Before leaving what is now Gaspé Bay, Cartier placed on the shore a large wooden cross and a shield bearing the fleur-de-lis emblem of France. Cartier and his men returned to France. Two native men went with them.

Who Were the Micmacs?

The Micmacs were the largest and most important native group occupying the maritime provinces of Canada in the fifteenth and sixteenth centuries. They lived in what is now Nova Scotia, New Brunswick, and Prince Edward Island. Early sources describe them as fierce and warlike, but they were the first natives to accept Christianity from French missionaries. The word *Micmac* means allies and the group was a confederacy of several clans. Each clan had its own symbols and chief. They were seminomadic, hunting moose and other wild game in the winter, while in the summer they fished along the coast and hunted sea mammals. During the winter they lived in wigwams covered with bark and skins. In the summer, they lived in open-air dwellings made from poles and branches. Micmacs dressed in loincloths, loose dresses, and robes. The robes were frequently decorated with fringe. They were noted for their ability as canoeists. Almost nothing is known about their rituals and religious beliefs.

King Francis was not deterred by the fact that Cartier did not find any precious metals or other commodities. Another voyage was authorized immediately. The purpose of this second voyage seems to have been to penetrate inland to the land of Canada. This time Cartier received a much larger fleet of three ships: the *Grand Hermine,* the *Petite Hermine,* and the *Emerillon.* The ships were supplied for fifteen months and carried a crew of about 112 as well as the two natives who had gone to France with Cartier. The plan was to sail inland and spend the winter in the land of Canada. Cartier and his crews sailed on May 19, 1535, arrived back at Anticosti Island on July 26, and immediately sailed on westward to an Iroquois village called Stadacona, located near present-day Quebec City.

Who Were the Iroquois?

Iroquois is a broad description of many native tribes whose territory ranged from the Great Lakes to the eastern seaboard of North America. They all spoke related languages. Iroquois groups practiced agriculture, fortified their villages, and lived in longhouses that would contain several families. The men generally hunted and traveled after game or traveled to fight battles. The women raised corn (maize), beans, and squash. In the spring, many families would travel to the coasts for extended fishing trips. Relationships were complicated among Iroquois groups since extended families lived together in longhouses. Families were organized into larger clans, and clans were organized into tribes, and tribes were united through confederacies. Each village had a chief who was advised by a council of adult males. Their oral literature is filled with myths about creation and the afterlife. Warfare was a constant fact of life because young men achieved personal glory and prestige through fighting. The Iroquois had by far the most complex social structure of the early peoples encountered by North American explorers.

The Iroquois discouraged Cartier from going any farther inland, but he proceeded with one ship, the *Emerillon*, leaving the other two ships and crews at Stadacona to build a fort for the winter. By September, they had anchored the *Emerillon* and proceeded by longboats farther up the river, arriving at the village of Hochelaga, near Mont-Royal, on October 2, 1535. The village of Hochelaga

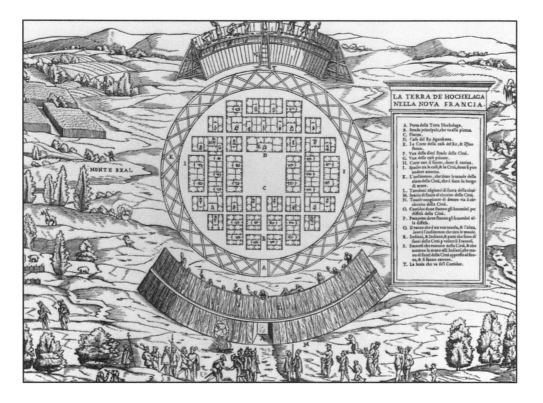

Village of Hochelaga based on Cartier's description as drawn by G. B. Ramusio in *Navigationi et Viaggi* (Venice, 1556). Some important sites according to the key to the map are as follows:

A. Gate to city of Hochelaga

B. The main street

C. The plaza

D. House of the king (or chief)

K. & L. Palisades

and nearby Mont-Royal would someday become the site of the modern-day city of Montreal. Jacques Cartier described his reception by the people of Hochelaga:

> So soon as we were near Hochelaga, there came to meet us about a thousand persons, men, women and children, who afterward did as friendly and merrily entertain and receive us as any father would do his child, which he had not of long time seen. The men dancing on one side, the women on another, and likewise the children on another. After that they brought us great stores of fish and of their bread made of millet.[2]

Jacques Cartier and some of his men climbed Mont-Royal with native guides. From the top they could see for miles. It became clear that the St. Lawrence River was not a passage to Asia, but the natives implied that gold and silver could be found farther to the west, following the St. Lawrence River into what they called the Land of Saguenay. Because winter was coming on, Cartier and his men could go no farther. They returned to Stadacona.

His crews at Stadacona had built a fort and all the Europeans settled in for the harshest winter any of them had ever experienced. To make matters worse, many of the men came down with sickness. Cartier's description of the illness clearly points to scurvy, which was just becoming known to Europeans at that time. Scurvy became a noticeable medical condition when longer ocean voyages were made without fresh foods to eat.

> Some did lose all their strength and could not stand on their feet, then did their legs swell, their sinews shrink as black as any coal. . . . Their mouth became stinking, their gums so rotten that all the flesh did fall off, even to the roots of the teeth, which did also almost all fall out.[3]

2. Henry Biggar, *The Voyages of Jacques Cartier* (Ottowa: Public Archives of Canada Publication No. 11, 1924), 152.
3. Henry Biggar, 162.

Another problem also plagued them. Friction between the French and the natives of Stadacona increased and a confrontation seemed imminent. In an effort to avoid open warfare, Cartier invited the chief, Donnacona, aboard his ship just before he was ready to sail back to France. Once the chief was aboard, Cartier refused to release him and forced him to accompany them. The natives of Stadacona were furious but there was little they could do. To ease the situation, Cartier pacified Donnacona with gifts and the promise to return him to his village the following year. Cartier set sail for France on May 6 and landed back at Saint-Malo on July 16.

Jacques Cartier and his men had achieved a great deal on this voyage. They had penetrated farther into the North American continent than anyone else from Europe, and they had established lasting contacts with native peoples. But they had not found the material wealth for which they had hoped. Nevertheless, the mistaken information they had received about gold and silver farther west had encouraged them to believe that such wealth existed. Chief Donnacona stimulated their imagination even more. Falsely, he described a land west of Hochelaga as a place where the natives dressed like the French, wore precious jewels, mined gold and silver, and collected spices. King Francis believed Chief Donnacona's stories, but it would take five years before he was able to finance another voyage.

The third expedition sponsored by the king and led by Jacques Cartier spared no expense. Ten ships with four hundred sailors and three hundred soldiers were prepared. Supplies were laid on board for a two-year stay, this time including the basics for building a permanent outpost in the land of Canada. Unfortunately, this expedition was a disaster.

An aristocrat by the name of Jean Francois de la Roche was to accompany Cartier as the governor of the new fort, but he was not able to organize his part of the expedition. Delay followed delay until finally, on May 23, 1541, Cartier left without him and with only five of the promised ships. He also took Donnacona along to return him to his people. Storms in the Atlantic were so bad that it took nearly three months to cross. They were nearly out of drinking water when they finally arrived at Stadacona on August 23.

Fortified dwellings were begun immediately for the men to live in during the long winter. As the workmen began building, they found stones that looked like gold and silver ore, and others that looked like diamonds. They dug the ore and loaded the ships with it. Cartier took two ships on up the river to Hochelaga, explored beyond it a few miles, and returned to Stadacona for the winter. It seemed that they had found their treasure, and it was evident that the natives were growing less friendly and probably planned to attack the fortress. In the spring, when the ice melted, Cartier loaded his ships and sailed back to France a year early.

Renaissance Maps of the North Atlantic

Renaissance maps of the North Atlantic relied on the stories and ideas of men such as Sebastian Cabot, the Côrte Real brothers, or Giovanni da Verrazano. Important mapmakers such as Abraham Ortelius encouraged explorers in their quest for a Northwest Passage by drawing configurations of the Arctic region which were highly inaccurate. Ortelius, for example, extended North America only as far as the St. Lawrence River. The rest of the landmass, as we know it, became the Arctic Ocean, forming an easy passage across to the Pacific Ocean. Ortelius was one of the most important mapmakers of his day and his ideas and maps greatly influenced European thinking during the sixteenth century.

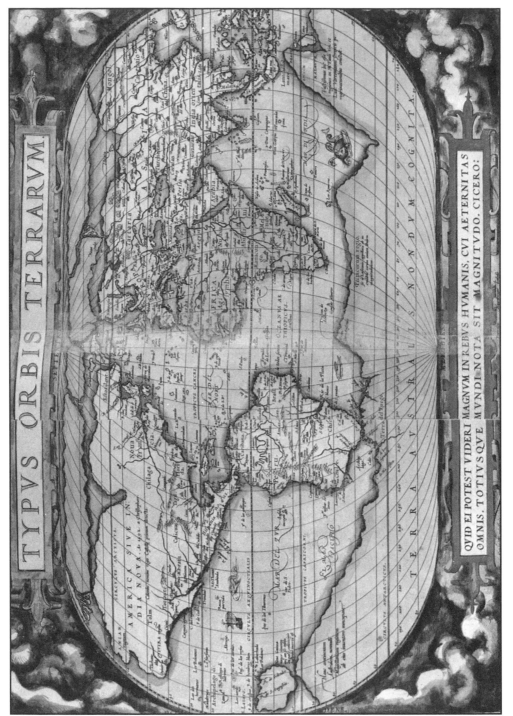

The Ortelius Map of 1564 shows the hoped-for Northwest Passage.

Cartier returned to France with great excitement because he believed that he had brought back precious stones and metals. But when they proved to be worthless, King Francis lost interest in the New World and refused to finance any more expeditions. We know almost nothing about Jacques Cartier's later life except that he was held in high regard by the French until he died in 1557. His explorations would not be important until long after he died, when the French government used them as their claim to Canada against the English.

After four decades of Europeans exploring the coastlines of the vast continents of the Western Hemisphere, North America seemed to many to offer the best possibility for a passage through that landmass to the Pacific Ocean and on to the Orient. Sebastian Cabot, who you will remember had been pilot major of Spain, had declared that he had found the entrance to such a passage in 1508. Such information, coming from an important government official, mapmaker, and explorer, excited people's imaginations and caused them to begin searching for the so-called Northwest Passage.

The search for a passage across the top of the North American continent would hold the attention of European explorers for nearly four hundred years. Belief that a waterway existed between the Atlantic and Pacific Oceans resulted from mythology, intellectual speculation, misleading data gathered from early explorers, and scientific fact. Such a passage does exist, as does a northeastern passage across the top of Russia and Siberia. What the early explorers did not know was that both passages are icebound. It would not be until the late nineteenth century that anyone actually crossed the Northwest Passage, and that was with great difficulty. It was not until the twentieth century that the trip became easier with nuclear submarines that traveled under the arctic ice.

The image that explorers hold of unknown lands is a composite of what they hope to find there, what they look for, and how what is actually found fits into the existing framework of knowledge. It is difficult initially to accept that all the

Two Famous Explorers Who Later Searched for the Northwest Passage

Perhaps the two most famous explorers who searched for the Northwest Passage in the sixteenth and seventeenth centuries were Martin Frobisher and Henry Hudson.

Frobisher's voyages were sponsored by a group of investors who hoped to locate the passage and control trade with China. The company was called the Company of Cathay. They hired Martin Frobisher, the well-known sea captain and suspected pirate, to lead the expedition. In 1576, in two ships with thirty-five men, Frobisher set out to locate the passage. He sailed into what we now know as Hudson Strait and began to explore that region until he found what he thought was gold ore. He returned with his find and the company financed another trip in 1577. This time he collected around two hundred tons of rock that he thought was gold and brought it back. The rock turned out to be pyroxenite and amphibolite (fool's gold), which was worthless. Nevertheless, the investors thought he was on to a large gold strike and financed a third voyage for him. This time, he tried to establish a mining colony on Baffin Island. It failed because of frequent native Inuit attacks. The failure to find real gold caused the Company of Cathay to go bankrupt, ending Frobisher's voyages. Archaeological excavations of Frobisher's colony on Baffin Island began in 1993.

Henry Hudson's name is almost synonymous with the Northwest Passage search. In 1607, Hudson tried without success to sail up Davis Strait and over the North Pole. In 1609, he was hired by the Dutch East Indies Company to find the Northwest Passage. His Dutch crews, however, did not like the Arctic and forced him to sail southward, where he explored the river that now bears his name—the Hudson River in New York. His report about this region was so enthusiastic that it was instrumental in encouraging the Dutch colony of

New Amsterdam, now New York City, to be situated at the mouth of that river. In 1610-11, Hudson entered the bay that today bears his name and explored that vast area. This was Hudson's most significant voyage in search of the Northwest Passage, and it was his last.

authorities are wrong, or that one's carefully thought out notions about a place are incorrect. From the time of John Cabot's first voyage in 1497 until 1845, over 140 ships and a few overland trips tried and failed to locate the Northwest Passage, which everyone believed to exist. It was not until Roald Amundsen's icebreaker the *Gjoa* successfully sailed the passage in 1903-1906 that the search was concluded.

In the sixteenth century, men explored the Arctic for commercial reasons— to find the Northwest Passage to the Orient. The Portuguese dominated the southeast route to Asia and the coast of Africa as well as a part of South America (Brazil). The Spanish controlled the land and sea from southern North America through the Caribbean, Mexico, and much of South America. Everyone else had to find another course if they wished to trade with the Orient. For the English and the French, the northern Atlantic seemed the most logical route left to them. But the search did not end when the passage was no longer needed for commercial reasons. In the eighteen and nineteenth centuries, men searched for the water-way for the mere prestige of finding it. In the nineteenth century, the quest centered on the national sovereignty of Canada. In the twentieth century, the exploration of the Arctic continued for reasons of national security for the North American nations in their cold war with the Soviet Union, and also as those nations prospected for mineral resources.

Four centuries of searching for the Northwest Passage took a great toll in men and equipment. The Arctic Ocean is filled with great ice floes that toss fifty-ton blocks of ice one on top of the other. The crushing and pushing of ice trapped has destroyed many vessels. Numerous sailors froze to death, or at best had to have arms, feet, and legs amputated because of frostbite.

In North America Europeans found no great cities or advanced civilizations as they had in South America. Nor did they find gold or silver or spices. The Northwest Passage remained a dream. Soon, though, the English, the French, and others began to appreciate what North America had to offer. All along, the explorers had described the rich natural resources of the region. Timber and fish were in high demand in Europe, and European fashion would soon make for a thriving trade in furs. The climate in North America was not much different than that of northern Europe.

By the turn of the seventeenth century coastal outposts and way stations were established to cultivate trade with the native people of North America. It was then a short step to the next stage of development: colonization. During the next century, European governments came to realize the potential of North American settlements as economic extensions of Old World countries. Thus, the next stage of the story is one of immigration, exploitation, and conflict.

GLOSSARY

Ancient: The time period in European history before the fall of the Roman Empire, usually calculated from the beginning of written records (around 3500 B.C.) to A.D. 500.

Anthropology: The study of the races, characteristics, distribution, customs, social relationships, etc., of mankind, including the study of the institutions and myths of primitive and extinct peoples.

Archives: Repositories of written documents and records from the past. Archives are found mostly in libraries and government offices and among families.

Artifacts: Any material remains of a culture or civilization that were made by human hands.

Bay: A part of the sea indenting the shoreline. Often applied to water around which the land forms a curve, such as Hudson Bay.

Bilge: The inside lower part of a ship's hull or hold.

Cape: Land jutting into a body of water beyond the rest of the coastline.

Cartography: The skill and art of making maps and charts.

Classical: 1. The age of greatness in Greek and Roman art, literature, and learning. 2. Greek and Roman forms in music, literature, art, science, etc., which became standard and authoritative in the ancient world. Such forms were greatly admired during the Renaissance period of European history.

Cosmography: The science dealing with the structure of the universe and its parts and combining astronomy, geography, and geology.

Demography: The science of vital statistics of populations either in the present or in the past.

Ethnography: A branch of anthropology that deals specifically with primitive peoples or groups.

Eurasia: The single landmass of Europe and Asia stretching between the Atlantic Ocean and the Pacific Ocean.

Fjord (fiord): A narrow inlet of the sea bordered by steep cliffs.

Geography: The science of the surface of the earth, including topography, cartography, physical environments, climates, inhabitants, etc.

Grand Banks: An area in the Atlantic Ocean south of Newfoundland where an undersea elevation rises from the continental shelf. These banks near Canada are one of the best fishing areas in the world.

Gunwale: 1. The upper edge of a ship's side. 2. A piece of timber which goes around the top side of a ship.

Iceberg: A large mass of ice broken off from a glacier and floating in the ocean.

Ice Floe: A great mass or sheet of floating ice on the ocean.

Ice Pack: A large expanse of floating ice, pressed and frozen together.

Isthmus: A narrow strip of land which connects two larger bodies of land.

Keel: The main foundation beam of a ship, running from stem to stern along the bottom and supporting the entire frame of the ship.

Landfall: Term referring to the sighting of land after a long ocean voyage.

Lateen Sail: Triangular-shaped sail.

Latitude: The angular distance on the globe north or south of the equator. Latitude is measured in degrees, with the equator being zero degree and each pole eighty degrees.

Maritime: This is a term related to a country, area, or people located next to the sea. It is also used to describe the characteristics of those who sail the seas.

Middle Ages (Medieval): The period in European history between ancient and modern times, usually calculated as between A.D. 500 and A.D. 1450.

Mizzenmast: The mast which stands nearest the stern of a ship.

Myth: Myths are traditional stories told over and over by people in any culture or civilization to explain such things as some feature of nature, the origin of man, his institutions, religion, rituals, and customs. Sometimes they have a historical basis and usually they are of unknown authorship.

Ocean Sea: The name of the Atlantic Ocean in ancient and medieval times. It was also called the Sea of Darkness. People believed that the Ocean Sea encircled all the landmass of the world.

Patent: A legal document from the government (or king) authorizing a trip of exploration and defining the rights of the holder of the patent.

Pillars of Hercules: The mythical Greek name for the entrance to the Mediterranean Sea. Today it is called the Rock of Gibralter.

Provisions: Used here, this refers to the supplies taken aboard a ship of exploration.

Relics: Material remains from the past, such as an arrow, a cup, or a piece of clothing. Anything man-made or man-used from a past era of history is a relic.

Renaissance: The name of a particular time period in history during the fourteenth, fifteenth, and sixteenth centuries which represents a revival of art, literature, and learning in Europe. Renaissance is a French word meaning "rebirth." The period is seen by historians as a transitional age between the Middle Ages (or medieval period) and the modern age.

Rigging: All the ropes and materials that support the masts and sails of a ship.

Rudder: A broad, flat, movable device hinged vertically at the stern of a ship and used for steering. Before the stern rudder was devised, any object used to guide or control a ship.

Sound: This name can be applied to a channel linking two bodies of water, to water separating an island from the mainland, or to a long inlet or arm of the sea.

Strait: A narrow waterway connecting two large bodies of water.

Terra Incognita: Latin term for unknown lands or areas on the map where no one had gone. Thus, it was unknown only to those who had not been there.

Topography: The science of drawing on maps and charts the surface features of any region.

FOR FURTHER READING

Baity, Elizabeth. *Americans Before Columbus*. New York: Viking Press, 1964.

Brown, Warren. *The Search for the Northwest Passage.* New York: Chelsea House, 1990.

Jacobson, Timothy. *Discovering America: Journeys in Search of the New World.* Toronto: Key Porter Books, 1991.

Morison, Samuel. *The Great Explorers.* New York: Oxford University Press, 1978.

Quinn, David. *England and the Discovery of America, 1481-1620.* London: Allen & Unwin, 1974.

Sharp, James. *Discovery in the North Atlantic.* Halifax: Nimbus Publishing, 1991.

Williamson, James. *The Voyages of the Cabots and the Discovery of North America.* New York: Harper and Row, 1970.

Wilson, Ian. *The Columbus Myth: Did Men of Bristol Reach America Before Columbus?* London: Simon & Schuster, 1991.

INDEX

Page numbers for illustrations are in italics.